Dear Diary,

How I wish this day could last forever! I've been so truly blessed to have my whole family with me this Christmas. Seeing them all gathered around my table, each one happily married and with growing families of their own, fills my heart with joy. What more could a mother want for her children?

The Lords arrived this evening to share in the celebration. Garrett, Michael, Lana and Shelby are as dear to me as my own family. They're all married now, too, except for Garrett. He remains stubbornly single, and seems more determined than ever to find his birth mother. If only...no, I cannot betray a promise. But I can make a special Christmas wish...

Fugitive Fiancée
KRISTIN GABRIEL

SILHOUETTE®
SPECIAL EDITION™

*First published in Great Britain 2004
Silhouette Books, Eton House, 18-24 Paradise Road,
Richmond, Surrey TW9 1SR*

© Harlequin Books S.A. 2000

Kristin Gabriel is acknowledged as the author of this work.

ISBN 0 373 65077 9

23-0504

*Printed and bound in Spain
by Litografia Rosés S.A., Barcelona*

KRISTIN GABRIEL

is a transplanted city girl who now lives on a farm in central Nebraska with her husband, three children, a springer spaniel and assorted cats. She received a BS in agriculture from the University of Nebraska before pursuing her dream of writing. Twice winner of the prestigious RITA® Award for Best Traditional Romance of the Year, Kristin is the author of nine books for Silhouette. Her first novel, *Bullets Over Boise*, was even turned into a made-for-television film called *Recipe for Revenge*. Kristin enjoys hearing from her readers and can be reached through her website at www.KristinGabriel.com, or at Kristin Gabriel, PO Box 5162, Grand Island, NE 68802-5162, USA.

CHAPTER ONE

GARRET LORD needed to find a place to hide. Fast. Caught between the corral and the old red barn, he could see the shiny blue Ford pickup truck rattling down the long gravel drive that led to his ranch house. The dual tires kicked up a plume of thick Texas dust that hovered in the fading twilight.

He only had a few precious seconds to take cover before he was spotted. He considered diving into the water trough by the corral, but he didn't think he could hold his breath for that long.

That left the barn.

He spun on the heel of his cowboy boot and bolted for the barn door, whipping it shut behind him just as he heard the sound of gravel crunching under the truck's tires. Hubert, his aspiring cow dog, began barking, alerting his master to the new arrival. But Garrett didn't have to worry about the little black schnauzer disclosing his hiding place. That dog was loyal through and through.

Too bad Garrett couldn't say the same about some of the people in his life.

He'd learned that lesson early. At two and a half years old, to be exact. When his mother had abandoned him and his younger sisters and brother. He couldn't even remember her. Not the color of her eyes, or her hair, or the sound of her laughter. When he was a young boy, he used to look for her on the streets and in department stores, certain he'd recognize his own mother when he saw her.

But it had never happened.

Now he was both older and wiser. He didn't indulge in childish fantasies anymore. It had taken him a while, long enough for another woman to rip away a little piece of his heart when she'd left him stranded at the altar seven years ago. She'd made a fool of him. But when the embarrassment had lasted longer than the heartache, he knew he'd gotten lucky. And he was smart enough not to make the same mistake twice.

Garrett always went with the odds, and love was definitely a long shot. Especially with his track record. Not to mention the astronomical divorce rate these days. Besides, he was more than content living alone. Working alone. Although he did treasure the time he spent with his sisters and brother. Time that was increasingly scarce now that Shelby, Lana and Michael had families of their own. As their older brother, he'd watched over the triplets for as long as he could remember. But they didn't need his protection anymore.

Now, if he could just find someone to protect him from man-hungry cowgirls.

He leaned toward the door, pressing one eye against a tiny crack in the wood. He could see the front porch and the young woman from the neighboring ranch who stood at the door. Venna held a large covered basket in one hand. No doubt another food offering to entice him into matrimony. Only food wasn't the way to Garrett's heart. Neither was her eclectic artwork. Last week she'd given him a painting of a clown to hang in his living room. He hated clowns.

As he slanted his head for a better view, Garrett suddenly realized that he'd been reduced to hiding from a woman. But it was that or endure Venna's incessant chatter until the wee hours of the morning again. She could talk almost as well as she could cook. And she was forever finding excuses to touch him.

She reminded him of a cat that had wandered onto his ranch a few years ago. Garrett was allergic to cats, so he'd avoided it as much as possible, leaving food and water in the barn, but keeping his distance. But the more he tried to keep away from it, the more the cat sought him out. Rubbing against his boots. Sleeping in his saddle. Leaving cat dander everywhere. When his sneezing and itchy, watery eyes had finally proven too much to bear, he'd foisted the overly affectionate feline on Mcgan Maitland. She'd always been good at taking in strays.

If only he could get rid of Venna as easily.

"Damn," he breathed as he watched her try the doorknob, then enter the house. He'd left the door unlocked and a light on in the living room, as well as a slow cooker full of beef stew simmering in the kitchen. All signs that might encourage her to wait for his return. Which meant he could be stuck in the barn for most of the evening.

He turned away from the door and strode down the center aisle of the barn. None of the six horses even gave him a glance, recognizing his familiar step. They stood in their wooden stalls, three on either side of the aisle, chewing contentedly on their evening ration of oats.

"At least the animals on this ranch get to eat," he muttered, his stomach rumbling. He climbed the plank ladder that led to the hayloft, figuring he might as well catch a few winks on a soft bed of straw while he waited. It beat staying awake and listening to his stomach growl.

The flutter of birds' wings and admonishing squawks greeted him. No doubt his presence disturbed some of the nesting barn swallows, who didn't like anyone invading their home.

He knew just how they felt.

"Hope you don't mind if I join you," he called to the birds as he reached the top of the ladder.

"Not at all."

Startled, Garrett lost his grip on the ladder and almost toppled off. When he regained his balance, he stared slack-jawed at the vision in front of him. Sitting atop a stack of golden straw was a bride.

He blinked and looked again. It was a bride, all right. He recognized all the warning signs—the white wedding dress, the gauzy fingertip veil, the white satin spiked heels on her dainty feet. Not to mention the lacy blue garter belt, revealed by the voluminous taffeta skirt bunched up around her thighs.

Before he could get a good look, she hastily pushed her skirt down, concealing the garter belt as well as a pair of long, slender legs.

For one brief moment, Garrett had an irrational impulse to shinny down the ladder and make a run for it. But run where? The house wasn't safe, and he'd be spotted out in the open. Besides, this was his ranch.

His barn. His hayloft. If anyone was leaving, it was the bride.

He climbed the last two rungs, then stepped onto the loft floor. Without giving the woman another glance, he sidled over to the dusty window and looked down at the driveway. The pickup was still there. Hubert was there, too, dutifully marking all the tires.

"You're probably wondering what I'm doing here," she said, breaking the long silence between them. Her voice was smooth and soft, like a warm, gentle breeze.

"I can guess." He clenched his jaw as he turned to face her. No doubt Shelby and Lana were to blame. His sisters had been hinting that his place needed a woman's touch ever since his housekeeper had retired. They'd brought up the subject again during Christmas dinner last week, even offering to play matchmaker for him.

Despite his irritation, he couldn't help but be impressed with their choice. Quality stock, no doubt about it. Tall and slender, with generous curves in all the right places. Her blond hair was swept up off her neck, a few errant strands curling around her cheeks. A tiara encircled the intricate bun on the top of her head, the tiny crystals sparkling in the fading sunlight.

She wore only a touch of makeup, and that was marred by the tiny smudge of dirt on her nose and another on her chin. The almost regal way she tilted that dirty chin made him want to smile. But she might take that as a sign of encouragement, which was the last thing he needed.

Then he made the mistake of looking into her eyes. Deep, blue eyes like the Texas sky after a storm. They held him. Captivated him. Something in his belly twisted, but he told himself it was just hunger pains. He'd been working since dawn, not bothering to stop for lunch. That explained the ache deep inside him. He needed food. Rest. He needed to be alone.

Garrett forced himself to look away from her as he brushed the dust off his denim jeans. "My sisters sent you here, didn't they?"

"No, I—"

"Then it must have been Michael," he muttered, rubbing one hand over his jaw. "Or Jake."

"Michael or Jake?" she echoed, looking perplexed.

"My brother and my *former* friend, if he's behind this." Michael Lord and Jake Maitland were once die-hard bachelors who had avoided marriage as vigorously as Garrett. But they had accidentally let down their guard, and two determined women had snatched them up. Of course, the fact that Garrett happened to like both their wives very much was beside the point.

Lately they'd been dropping broad hints that Garrett should follow in their footsteps. But a bride in his barn? So much for subtlety.

Only what the hell did he do with her now? If he kicked her out of his hayloft, it might call attention to his presence. Better to wait until the coast was clear.

"I believe I owe you an explanation, Mr...."

"Garrett." He bit the word out.

"Well, Mr. Garrett…"

"Just call me Garrett," he interjected. He didn't stand on formality. And even though he'd carried the Lord name for more than twenty-five years, lately it had only served to remind him that he'd had another last name once. A name he still didn't know.

"All right, Garrett. You may call me Mimi."

He wasn't planning on calling her anything, except a cab. Which made him wonder how she got way out here. He hadn't seen any strange cars around the place. Though his ranch was located only a few miles outside Austin, it was tucked deep in the hill country, accessible only by a winding backroad. Had she been en route to her wedding at some quaint country church and lost her way?

She certainly looked lost. Not only was she over-dressed for the barn, but her manicured fingernails and those dainty shoes on her feet told him she was completely out of her element. He studied her face, noting the creamy smooth complexion, which obviously hadn't seen any days working in the sun and wind. Her cheekbones were high, her nose finely shaped and tipped just slightly at the end. Her eyebrows and lashes were slightly darker than her hair, like burnished gold.

She licked her lips. "I know the last thing you expected to find up here was a bride sitting on your haystack."

He swallowed a groan. It was worse than he thought. Bad enough he'd found a bride in his barn. She was a city girl, to boot. "You're sitting on straw, not hay."

A golden brow lifted. "Really? What's the difference?"

"Wheat straw is yellow and used for livestock bedding. Hay is cut from grasses, like brome, and is fed to the stock. It's green, and your pretty white dress would be, too, if you were sitting on hay."

"I'm learning all kinds of fascinating things today," she said, her tone telling him she wasn't exactly thrilled about it.

Well, he wasn't thrilled, either. Not only was he stuck in the barn for who knew how long, he was stuck here with a city girl. A worried city girl, judging by the way her perfect teeth kept nipping that lush lower lip. Shadows clouded her blue eyes as she looked at him.

A vague uneasiness tightened his gut. Maybe this wasn't a prank. Maybe she wasn't lost. Maybe this woman was in trouble.

"If you'd just let me explain," Mimi began, winding her fingers together.

"That really isn't necessary." Garrett moved to the window. Despite his natural curiosity, he didn't want to know any details about her. Didn't want this woman to intrude on his life more than she already had. Those shadows in her eyes bothered him. If he found out how they got there, he might feel obliged to help her. And he had enough problems of his own to deal with right now.

It was better if they remained strangers. Better for him, anyway. Sometimes he wondered if that's why Jake Maitland had spent all those years working as a secret operative for the government. Moving from place to place had kept him from making ties and establishing relationships. Even his own family had rarely known how to find him. Maybe he'd liked it that way.

Because sometimes it hurt to care too much.

The creak of the barn door startled them both. Garrett whirled, locking eyes with Mimi. Her wary blue eyes widened at the sound of footsteps below them.

"Hide," Garrett ordered in a husky whisper, diving behind a tall stack of straw. Mimi rolled off her perch to join him there, tangling them both in a billowing cloud of white taffeta.

They both batted down her wayward skirts, then froze as a feminine voice called from below. "Anybody here?"

One of the horses whinnied in reply.

"Garrett?" Her shout startled the barn swallows perched high in the rafters, and they fluttered around their nests.

Garrett saw Mimi open her mouth, and he immediately clamped his hand over it. Her lips were soft and warm against his palm. He felt a touch of moisture, like dew, on his skin, when she tried to speak. He shook his head, his body tightening at the thought of her small pink tongue touching him, tasting him.

She looked at him with those blue eyes, then finally nodded slowly in understanding. He removed his hand, suddenly aware of how close Mimi was to him. He could feel the silky wisps of her blond hair tickling his cheek and the soft fullness of one breast pressed against his upper arm. She was so warm and so very, very soft. One of her legs had tangled with his during their fall, her creamy skin rubbing against the rough fabric of his jeans. He didn't dare move, even as a hot, tingling sensation shot through his veins to other parts of his body.

He looked into her eyes and found her still staring at him, their faces only a hairbreadth apart. He hadn't been this close to a woman in months—and his body was reminding him of that fact. His heart pounded, and his breathing hitched.

"Garrett?" The voice below called again, closer now. "Are you up there?"

His muscles tensed as his attention was drawn away from Mimi. He held his breath, letting it out slowly when he finally heard the sound of receding footsteps. The barn door creaked once again.

Venna was gone.

He immediately put a healthy distance between himself and the bride. That's when he noticed her hands were shaking.

"What's wrong?" he asked.

She swallowed hard and shook her head. "Nothing. I'm fine."

Without thinking, Garrett reached out and clasped her small hands in his. Her fingers were as cold as ice. "You're not fine."

He hauled her off the floor and began roughly brushing strands of golden straw from her wedding dress. The roar of an engine drew his gaze to the window. He watched with relief as the pickup peeled out of his driveway toward the country road. Then he turned to Mimi. "It's safe now. We can go to the house and you can call someone to pick you up."

"That's not necessary," she breathed. Her fingers clutched the skirt of her wedding dress so tightly her knuckles matched the pearly white fabric.

"Believe me, it is." He strode toward the ladder, then waited for her to follow.

She stayed rooted to the spot. "I can't leave."

"You can't stay," he countered, his tone registering his impatience.

She looked at him and licked her lips. Panic flared in her eyes. "You don't understand. I...I don't know where to go. I don't know what to do."

He heard the edge of desperation in her voice and moved closer to her. "It's all right," he said softly, using the same tone he used to gentle a spooked horse. "Everything will be all right. Come with me to the house. We'll figure out what to do."

Her tense shoulders relaxed a fraction. She took a deep breath, then gave him a shaky nod.

Garrett gently grasped her elbow and led her toward the ladder. She gathered her voluminous skirt in her hands, then carefully climbed down the wooden rungs. Her knees buckled when she reached the barn floor, and Garrett watched her grab on to a wooden support beam to steady herself. He jumped down the last few rungs and hurried to her side.

"I'm all right," she assured him. "I haven't eaten anything all day and the...excitement must be catching up with me."

Damn. Bad enough he'd found a citified bride stowed away in his barn. Now she was about to pass out from hunger. How could she leave his ranch if she was unconscious? Without bothering to ask her permission, Garrett bent and scooped her into his arms. He ignored her sharp gasp of protest as he gathered her close to his chest. A little closer than necessary. But he couldn't resist the urge to inhale her unique scent and feel all that softness against his body one last time.

His horse Brutus emitted a high-pitched whinny as

Garrett headed for the barn door, a sputtering bride in his arms. If he didn't know better, he'd think the big bay gelding was laughing at him.

AS SOON AS Garrett carried Mimi out of the barn, the wild Texas wind snatched at her veil and whipped it across his face. He spit three layers of tulle out of his mouth, then muttered an oath under his breath.

"You can put me down now," she said, more than a little unnerved by his brute strength. She weighed one hundred and thirty pounds, and the man wasn't even breathing hard.

"This is my ranch," he bit out, shifting her slightly in his arms as he strode toward the house. "I'm the one who gives the orders."

Mimi clenched her jaw and held her tongue. She couldn't afford to antagonize him. She couldn't keep staring at him, either. It wasn't proper for a woman who'd almost married another man less than four hours ago. And Mimi Casville had been raised to be a proper young lady. To behave perfectly in every social situation. She'd always tried to follow the rigid dictates of high-society etiquette.

Until today.

Running out of your own wedding was not considered polite behavior in Austin society. Or anywhere else, for that matter. A well-bred, proper young lady did not abandon her groom at the altar. Or leave four hundred guests crowded together in the overly warm sanctuary.

But Mimi had done exactly that. And now she was in the arms of a cowboy. A very handsome cowboy who was partly to blame for the weakness in her knees and the erratic beat of her heart. She blinked at him, unable to look away. His face was tanned and rugged, testimony to long days working under the hot Texas sun. The shadow of stubble on his square jaw matched the russet hair almost hidden beneath his black felt cowboy hat.

Her cheeks blazed when his green-gold eyes caught her staring at him. She blinked and quickly looked away. But not before his gaze touched something in her soul. The way he looked at her... If her fiancé had ever looked at her that way, just once, she might be a married woman right now.

Mimi closed her eyes, pushing thoughts of her duplicitous fiancé out of her mind. She couldn't think about him. Not now. Instead, she leaned her head against Garrett's broad chest and focused her attention on the ranch house.

It was a rustic, two-story stone-fronted structure, fifty years old or so, but well-maintained. Black shutters accented every window, and small wisps of smoke curled out of the stone chimney. An inviting wraparound porch held a porch swing and a small doghouse. Wood creaked as Garrett climbed the steps that led to his front door.

Like most girls, Mimi had always dreamed of her wedding day. In her mind's eye, she'd seen a magnificent cathedral full of friends and family. A reverent candlelight service. A handsome, adoring groom.

She sighed. So far, it hadn't turned out at all like she'd planned. She'd certainly never imagined being carried over the threshold by a cantankerous cowboy. Although the stranger holding her in his arms had a solidity about him that she'd rarely experienced before. A gentle strength that inexplicably made her want to nestle closer to him.

At least until he marched through the front door and dumped her on the beige leather sofa in his living room. Then he turned on his heel and left without a word.

Mimi lay there stunned for a moment, listening to the clomp of his cowboy boots in the next room. Then she struggled to sit up. It was difficult to do anything in her five-thousand-dollar wedding dress. One hundred and ten silk-covered buttons ran down the back of the dress from her neck to her tailbone. Steel ribbing cinched her middle like an old-fashioned corset. It made her waist look impossibly tiny and her breasts impossibly big. It also made it very hard to breathe. Little wonder she'd almost passed out.

When she finally managed to pull herself upright, she took a long look around the room. A sturdy oak coffee table separated the sofa from two oversize leather armchairs. A handwoven rug with rich hues of blue, green and burgundy stretched across the polished hardwood floor. Another rug lay in front of the stone hearth, where a small fire glowed. A rustic Christmas wreath made of fragrant pine boughs still hung over the mantel.

She leaned back against the sofa, listening to the crackle and snap of the fire and watching the shadows of the flames dance on the wall.

Mimi's instincts told her Garrett was definitely a bachelor. There were no fussy feminine touches in the room, although she found she liked the Spartan simplicity surrounding her. It was an improvement over the ostentatious Colonial-style mansion she'd grown up in.

Tears pricked her eyes. She might never see that home again. Never see her father, who was no doubt bullying his way through Austin right now searching for her. Her throat grew so tight it was almost painful. She couldn't let him find her. Not until she had time to straighten out the mess she'd made of her life.

The day seemed like a blur. Or rather like a nightmare. One you couldn't escape by waking up. It was all too real. The betrayal and the lies. The careful scheming and the furtive whispers. All designed to make Mimi believe an illusion. Only now her eyes were wide open.

She'd never been this alone before. No, that wasn't true. Once. Just once she'd been even more frightened, more desperate. It was a time she didn't like to think about. A time that made her heart ache. *Ten years ago.* She closed her eyes and swallowed her tears. Now wasn't the time to reminisce about lost hopes and broken dreams. She had to stay strong. Had to figure a way out of this mess.

After taking several deep breaths, Mimi opened her eyes, more composed. She couldn't worry about the past or the future. Right now the present demanded all her energy.

Garrett entered the room carrying a tray with two steaming wooden bowls on it and a crusty loaf of bread. He set it on the coffee table, then handed her one of the bowls. "Eat every drop."

Mimi sat up and reached for the spoon, assuming this to be another one of his orders. She was much too hungry to think about disobeying it. The savory aroma of the stew made her mouth water. She spooned up a hearty bite, blew gently on it, then put it in her mouth, closing her eyes in appreciation as the delicious flavors mingled on her tongue.

"This is wonderful," she said, spooning up another bite. It seemed so peaceful somehow, eating stew with a perfect stranger. Away from all the pressures that had built around her for the past few weeks.

"Anything tastes good when you're half-starved." He sliced a thick slab of bread from the loaf and handed it to her.

So Garrett didn't take orders or compliments well, Mimi thought as she watched him cut a slice of bread for himself. He didn't take kindly to finding stray brides in his barn, either, judging by his earlier reaction.

He looked up and caught her staring at him again. "Eat."

Her cheeks warmed, and she immediately dropped her gaze to her bowl. She sensed that Garrett, like his adorable dog, was all bark and no bite. The little black schnauzer had growled ferociously at her when she'd first stepped foot on the ranch. Of course, the pup had ruined his guard-dog act by licking her ankles and rolling over on his back for a belly rub.

Not that his master could be so easily pacified. An unbidden image of Garrett licking her ankles flashed in her mind, and Mimi choked on her stew. Heat washed up her face as Garrett looked at her.

"Are you all right?"

"Fine," she replied, hoping he'd blame the steaming stew for the fiery flush on her cheeks.

To make matters worse, he pushed away his empty

bowl, then leaned back in his chair and slowly rubbed one hand over his taut stomach. Maybe he enjoyed belly rubs as much as his dog.

She tried to swallow the giggle bubbling up her throat, but it erupted in a very unladylike snort. He scowled at her, and Mimi didn't know what to do. Laugh? Cry? Both seemed equally tempting at the moment.

But now was not the time to become hysterical. She could save her tears for later. It wasn't proper for a dinner guest to weep over her food. So instead she took a deep, calming breath and endeavored to make polite dinner conversation.

"This bread is delicious." Mimi had never baked bread in her life, but she knew after the first succulent bite that it was homemade. Still warm from the oven, the bread was crusty on the outside and tender on the inside.

"Venna made it."

"Venna?" Mimi wiped her buttery fingers on her paper napkin. "Is she your cook?"

"Nope."

She waited for him to elaborate, but he turned his gaze to the fireplace. His silence only made her more curious. Mimi wasn't naturally nosy, but for some reason, this man intrigued her more than most. Maybe because he didn't know anything about her or her illustrious family. He wasn't trying to impress her or charm her or do anything to draw himself closer to the Casville fortune.

He might even *like* her if he got to know her. Like her for herself, instead of what her family's money and power might do for him.

She spooned up more stew. "Then she must be your fairy godmother."

That got his attention. He turned his gaze from the fire to her. "What?"

"This mysterious Venna. I thought she might be some kind of fairy godmother who magically makes fresh-baked bread appear on your table every evening."

He scowled. "There's nothing mysterious about her. Venna Schwab was the woman in the barn."

"The woman you were hiding from?"

"I wasn't hiding," he said, not quite meeting her gaze. "I just don't happen to like unexpected company."

She chose to ignore the innuendo. "Why? I'd think a person would get pretty lonely way out here—with nothing but cows and coyotes to keep you company."

"That's the way I like it," he countered. "Although a ranch is no place for a city girl like you."

She blanched. "How did you know?"

"I can spot a city girl a mile away. Not many women out here waste money on a fancy manicure." He motioned to her polished pink fingernails. "Or wear silly shoes like the ones you've got on."

She lifted her feet a few inches off the floor. "These silly shoes happen to be imported from Italy. They're designer originals!"

"Well, they're not worth two bits out here. Between the dirt and the gravel and the scrub brush they'll be ruined in no time."

She shrugged and placed her feet on the floor. "I didn't have time to change. I left in rather a hurry."

She expected him to ask her why, but instead he

swept the bread crumbs off the coffee table into his empty bowl. Then he looked at her. "Finish your stew."

"Aren't you the least bit curious about me?" she asked, ignoring his latest order.

"No." He settled back in the armchair and folded his arms across his chest. "I've learned the hard way that curiosity can be a dangerous thing. Now, do you need a ride back into Austin, or did you drive out here?"

"I drove." She licked the last few bread crumbs off her fingers. "At least, until I ran out of gas. Then I walked."

He arched a brow. "Walked? In those shoes?"

"Of course not. I took them off and carried them."

He leaned forward. "You mean you walked barefoot on these gravel roads? Exactly how far did you go?"

She shrugged. "Five or six miles. I lost count."

He rose and moved toward her. Then he knelt in front of the sofa and picked up her foot. She winced as he carefully removed her right shoe.

"Damn," he breathed. Beneath the shredded sheer stocking, raw blisters and tiny cuts covered the sole of her foot. Without another word, he carefully pulled the stocking away from her skin, then ripped it apart with his powerful hands. It split all the way to her knee.

Mimi looked down to see that her pink pedicured toenails were torn, dirty and bleeding. Her head spun, and she reached out to grab his broad shoulder. She hated acting weak in front of him, but at the moment she was too busy trying not to pass out to care.

"What's wrong?" he asked, his callused hands cradling her foot.

"Nothing. It's silly."

"Tell me."

As Mimi struggled to remain conscious, she thought about all the money her father had wasted on doctors and even a hypnotist to help her overcome this ridiculous reaction to the sight of blood. Especially her own. But nothing had helped. In fact, her father's insistence that she conquer this weakness had only seemed to make it worse.

At last, she took a deep breath and focused her attention on his face instead of her foot. "The sight of blood makes me a little woozy. In fact, I have to wax my legs instead of shaving them because I'll pass out if I nick myself with a razor."

Heat flooded her face when she realized how inappropriate it was to tell him that intimate little detail. Especially now that his thumb was absently stroking the sleek, bare skin of her ankle.

She swallowed hard at his sensuous touch, wanting it both to stop and to go on forever. "I...you...I mean, this really isn't necessary."

"Don't look," he ordered as he turned his attention to her left foot.

She squeezed her eyes shut, but she couldn't stop the small gasp that left her lips when he tugged off her other shoe.

"Does that hurt?"

"Not really," she breathed, warily opening her eyes.

"Liar," he said softly. Then he stood, turned and tossed her shoes in the fireplace.

She watched in mute horror as her five-hundred-dollar shoes went up in flames. "What do you think you're doing?"

"I'm doing you a favor."

"But...those are the only shoes I have with me."

"My sister Shelby keeps a pair of boots here that she only wears when she comes out to ride." His gaze flicked over her. "Might not be a perfect fit, but you two look about the same size."

"That's not the point. You had no right to dispose of my property. How would you like it if I—" she motioned wildly toward the large picture window "—burned down your barn!"

He arched a brow. "Is that what you were planning to do in there?"

"Of course not. If you want to know the truth, I was hiding out. I figured a hayloft was the last place my fiancé would look, especially since he has horrible hay fever." She swallowed, realizing the time had come to tell him everything. Well, maybe not everything. She did have some pride.

"I was supposed to be married today. But I..." Mimi's voice quavered, and she paused a moment to gain control. "I just couldn't go through with it. So I left him at the altar, hopped into my car and drove until it wouldn't go any farther."

The memory rekindled her anger, making her voice stronger. "It didn't matter to me where or how far, I just had to get away. As far away as possible."

A muscle ticked in Garrett's jaw, but he didn't say anything.

"I walked until I couldn't take another step," she continued, her fingers flexing on the wrinkled skirt of her gown. "That's when I saw your ranch. There wasn't anyone around but the dog, and he seemed friendly enough. I thought I could rest for a while in your hayloft. Maybe even stay the night."

Garrett just stared at her.

"I know that was presumptuous. And I apologize for trespassing on your property." She nibbled her lower lip. "But I really didn't know what else to do. I certainly couldn't walk right into your house, unlocked or not."

She swallowed again, her throat dry. "I'd only been up in your hayloft for about thirty minutes when you arrived."

The way Garrett was looking at her made her increasingly uneasy. Raw emotion smoldered in his eyes.

"Well," she said after a long, uncomfortable silence, "don't you have anything to say?"

"Yes." His voice sounded low and tight. "Get the hell off my ranch."

CHAPTER TWO

MIMI FLINCHED as the front door slammed. Garrett had ordered her to leave, but he'd been the one to stomp out the door. *Men.* She'd never understand them. Her father was just as unfathomable. Not to mention prickly and stubborn.

Today she'd also learned he was a liar.

Her chest tightened, and Mimi sat up straight on the sofa, suddenly unable to breathe. Frantic fingers clumsily worked the silk buttons running down the back of her gown. The fabric ripped, and she gasped for air until she was finally free of the confining garment.

She stood up, shimmying out of the voluminous gown and letting it pile at her feet. Then she stepped out of it, still decently covered from ankle to collarbone by her white silk bridal slip. She kicked the gown into the corner, then sat on the sofa, placing her head between her knees to regain her equilibrium.

Not a full-fledged panic attack, but close enough. A sign that her life was spinning out of control. Again. It had first happened when she was a freshman in college. A silly infatuation with a charming upperclassman had turned her life upside down and almost caused her to quit school.

Then, two years ago, her father had been diagnosed

with colon cancer. Mimi had immediately left her job with the Archives Department of the Houston Metropolitan Research Center and moved home, devoting herself to her widowed father's care.

An astute businessman, Rupert Casville was suddenly faced with his own mortality. His illness and frailty terrified Mimi.

He lost all interest in Casville Industries, leaving everything in the capable hands of his business attorney, Paul Renquist.

Without his business to occupy his time, her father had focused on continuing the Casville legacy. He soon became obsessed with having grandchildren, and since Mimi was his only child, it was up to her to provide them. Rupert's obsession only got worse after his remission.

She bit her lip, remembering her father's wistful pleas for a grandson. But despite her empathy for him, she'd kept her secret. A secret she'd carried for a decade. Still, a sense of guilt made her agree to go on an endless series of blind dates. But none of the self-absorbed, eligible bachelors her father had found appealed to her.

At twenty-eight, she no longer expected to find her soul mate. But she was willing to settle for someone she could depend on. A man who shared her desire for children and treated her with respect.

A man like Paul Renquist.

He was handsome and charming. A self-made man and a savvy attorney, Paul had efficiently handled every business crisis during her father's illness. Strong and steady, he had been a solid rock to cling to in her suddenly stormy life.

Still, his marriage proposal had come as a complete surprise. Mimi had been stunned, since they'd never shared more than a few casual dinner dates. Paul's reasons for a marriage between them had made so much sense. She hadn't stood a chance against his polished negotiating skills. Especially when he'd insisted on a prenuptial agreement that would prevent him from receiving any of the Casville millions if they divorced.

So Mimi had said yes, believing she'd eventually grow to love him.

Then today, thanks to the ancient ventilation system in the old cathedral, she'd discovered her father had been paying him to romance her all along. Mimi had been alone in the dressing room, fighting off another impending panic attack, when she'd heard their illuminating conversation through the air vent.

She liked to think it was divine providence.

She closed her eyes, her head spinning. She'd almost married a man she didn't love. Almost destroyed her own life, trying to please her father.

Fleeing her wedding was the first impulsive thing she'd done in her life. For the first time she could remember, she wasn't standing in the suffocating shadow of the Casville name. And Garrett was the first man who didn't see dollar signs when he looked at her.

Not that he wanted to look at her. The man had just ordered her out of his house. He obviously didn't realize she wasn't taking orders anymore.

Only she still wasn't sure what to do next.

A dull ache throbbed in her temple as she contemplated her options. No doubt her father and Paul had already started a full-scale search. She couldn't go home. She couldn't go to a hotel, either, since she didn't have any of her credit cards with her.

More than anything, Mimi needed time to heal. And what better place than on a secluded ranch in the starkly beautiful Texas hill country?

But first she had to figure out a way to convince Garrett to let her stay.

"WOMEN," Garrett muttered under his breath as he marched along the fence line, his way lit by the full moon. "I'll never understand them."

Hubert trotted beside him, emitting a tiny bark as he bounded forward to keep up with Garrett's long stride.

"It's like they go out of their way to drive a man crazy." Garrett looked at his dog. "Take my advice, Hubert. Don't ever get mixed up with some female. Even if she has eyes like the Texas sky and hair like clover honey."

Hubert yelped, then drew up his front paw and limped on three legs. Garrett bent and pulled a sand-bur from the tender pad of the dog's small paw. Then he straightened and leaned against the corral fence, propping one boot on the bottom rail.

He gazed at the canopy of stars glittering across the big Texas sky. "Of all the haylofts in all the world, why did she have to end up in mine?"

Hubert barked at him, wagging his cropped tail.

Garrett sighed, wondering when he'd become such a coldhearted son of a bitch. Ordering the woman off his ranch hadn't been one of his finer moments. He stared at the moonlit horizon, letting the nippy breeze cool his temper.

Women had plagued him all day. First his sister Lana, inviting him to dinner. Suspicious of the spark of mischief in her eye, he'd finally gotten her to confess that she planned to invite a date for him, as well. He'd turned down her invitation, but she hadn't made it easy. Lana could be almost as stubborn as Garrett when she set her mind to something.

Then Venna had come after him again, still hellbent on roping him into matrimony. He couldn't decide if she was incredibly determined or just delusional. The last thing he wanted was a woman looking for husband number three.

Then there was Mimi.

Mimi. Ever since he'd caught her in his hayloft, she'd been like a sandbur under his skin. Only she didn't cause him any pain. Far from it. She made him remember how damn long it had been since he'd held a woman in his arms. How soft and warm and wonderful women could be.

If only they weren't so damn much trouble.

He'd tried ignoring her, insulting her and intimidating her, but she hadn't taken the hint. He wanted her off his ranch and out of his life. If she wouldn't go willingly, then he'd fling her over his shoulder and haul her to Austin himself.

"Come on, Hubert," Garrett said, turning to the house. "Time to take Mimi back where she belongs."

He marched to the house and through the front door, ready to meet any resistance. But his resolve faded when he saw her curled up on the sofa, her eyes closed and her mouth slightly open. He pushed the door shut behind him, a little louder than necessary, but she didn't even stir.

Her wedding dress was in a heap on the floor. He moved closer to the sofa, noticing the shadows under her eyes. Then his gaze flicked to her bare feet, peeking out beneath the hem of her long silk slip. The raw scratches and livid welts on the soles of her feet looked even worse than before.

The fire popped in the hearth, shooting a spray of orange sparks and making shadows dance on the walls. Watching her sleep, Garrett wondered why he'd let her upset him so much. Mimi was no threat to him. She was some other man's problem. She was also in obviously desperate straits if she'd trust a total stranger not to take advantage of her. He doubted either of his sisters would ever end up in such a crazy situation, but if they did, he hoped no one would kick them out into the cold night.

Picking up the lonestar quilt off the back of the sofa, he gently draped it over her sleeping form, then he switched off the living room light.

"First thing in the morning," he vowed to himself. "She's outta here."

Austin American Statesman
WEDDING BELLE BLUES
Mimi Casville, daughter of prominent Austin industrialist Rupert Casville, ran out of St. Mary's Cathedral in Austin yesterday, just moments before she was to exchange vows with local attorney Paul Renquist.

The runaway bride wore a stunning gown of oyster silk with a sweetheart-style bodice and delicate spaghetti straps. Hand-sewn pearls accented the box-pleated skirt and cathedral train.

The groom, resplendent in a black cutaway coat and tails designed by the incomparable Oscar de la Renta, refused to comment. The champagne reception went on as scheduled, absent the unwedded couple. All four hundred guests dined on Rockefeller oysters, Russian caviar and juicy rumors regarding the fractured nuptials.

Official word is that the bride succumbed to a sudden illness and that the wedding will be rescheduled in the near future. Unofficially, sources say that the bride fled the scene in her red convertible and hasn't been seen since.

Destination of Ms. Casville unknown. Stay tuned to this column for further updates.

—Bettina Collingsworth

"DID YOU SEE this crap?"

Paul Renquist looked up from his breakfast plate as Rupert Casville marched into the formal dining room, waving a newspaper in his hand. Paul had spent the night at the Casville mansion, hoping to talk some sense into Mimi when she returned home.

Only she hadn't come home.

"It's in the society section, Rupert. Nobody who matters reads that."

"I sure as hell read it." Rupert slapped the newspaper on the polished oak table. "Who is this Bettina Collingsworth woman, anyway?"

"She reports all the high-profile weddings in Austin."

"Obviously, she missed her calling. She should be writing UFO reports for the tabloids." Rupert pulled out a chair and sat down at the table. "I can't believe a newspaper like the *Austin American Statesman* would print such melodramatic tripe. I'm tempted to buy the damn newspaper myself just so I can fire this dingbat."

Paul picked up his fork. "I called Mrs. Collingsworth this morning and asked her to print a retraction."

"And?"

"And she refused." Paul hesitated as a maid brought in Rupert's breakfast. Maria only spoke a few words of English, or at least that's what she claimed. Paul didn't believe in taking chances, so he kept his mouth shut.

"This looks wonderful, Maria," Rupert said, unfolding his napkin. "Thank you."

She nodded, then, with a dismissive glance at Paul, walked out of the room.

A hot flush crept up his neck. He hated the way the servants looked at him, as if he'd crawled into the Casville mansion on his belly. He'd put his foot down when Mimi had wanted to invite them to the wedding.

Was that why she'd left him at the altar?

He shook his head, still baffled by her behavior. For the last six months, he'd bent over backward to accommodate her every need, grant her every wish. He'd even agreed to her outrageous request not to consummate their relationship until the wedding night.

What more did she want?

Rupert reached for the salt and pepper, liberally sprinkling his plate with both. He ate the same breakfast every morning. Three eggs over easy, a rasher of bacon, hominy grits and a big glass of tomato juice. "So what else did she say?"

Paul looked at him. "Who?"

"That Collingsworth dame."

Paul picked up a spoon and returned his attention to his grapefruit. "She told me she witnessed Mimi running out of the church herself. So she didn't buy our story about the bride suddenly taking ill."

"Damn." Rupert reached into his suitcoat and pulled out a small silver flask. He unscrewed the lid, then poured a generous shot of vodka into his tomato juice.

Paul swallowed hard, his throat suddenly very dry. "I'll take one of those."

Rupert raised a grizzled brow. "I thought you gave up the booze."

"Hell, Rupert, my bride's run out on me! I can't think of a better occasion to fall off the wagon, can you?"

Rupert set the flask on the table and pushed it toward him. "There you go, Paul. Enjoy. Of course, you take one drink, and you can forget about ever marrying my daughter."

Paul froze, his hand already outstretched toward the flask. He glanced at Rupert's slate-blue eyes and instinctively knew he meant business. But then, Rupert Casville always meant business. And he never let inconsequential things like friends or family, or even his only daughter, stand in his way.

"Marry her?" Paul's hand curled into a fist as he slumped in his chair. "We can't even find her."

"Mimi simply got a case of cold feet. She'll be back." Rupert took a sip of tomato juice. "Her mother was skittish, too. High-strung. The thorough-breds always are."

Paul watched Rupert push his food away, half-eaten. He'd lost a considerable amount of weight in the last two years. Of course, Rupert's loss was Paul's gain. His illness had given Paul a golden opportunity for a more powerful role at Casville Industries. Not only had he succeeded in a professional sense, but he'd impressed Rupert enough for the CEO to consider him husband material for his man-shy daughter.

Rupert tossed his linen napkin on the table. "I still can't believe Mimi didn't come home last night. It's not like her to be so irresponsible."

"I suppose we just need to be patient."

"Patient?" Rupert snapped. "I didn't become one of the richest men in Texas by sitting around on my backside. I make things happen."

Paul clenched his jaw, willing himself to keep his mouth shut. He'd been doing a damn good job of it for the last two years, working by Rupert's side and patiently enduring the man's patronizing attitude and all-around bullshit day after day.

Now, thanks to Mimi's little stunt, he'd have to put up with it even longer. He closed his eyes and imagined wringing her beautiful neck. Not that he'd ever follow through, of course. When she finally made an appearance, he'd act the part of the concerned, supportive fiancé, assuring her that this marriage would be good for both of them. Just as he'd been doing almost nonstop for the last three months.

The funny thing was, he almost believed it himself. Mimi was an attractive, vivacious woman who would make a wonderful wife. She knew all the right people and moved in all the right circles. Her basic goodness appealed to him, even when he found himself grating his teeth at her concern for her father and the household staff.

Her only concern should be him.

"The girl's probably just hiding out somewhere, too embarrassed to come home." Rupert picked up his tomato juice. "As soon as you're done with breakfast, I want you to hire someone to find her."

"It's already done." Paul set down his fork. "I called Harper first thing this morning."

Rupert nodded approvingly. "He's the best."

"Discreet, too," Paul added, then hesitated. "Do you think she found out about our...financial agreement?"

"How could she? I certainly didn't say anything."

"Neither did I. So there must be some reason for her sudden departure from the church."

Rupert set down his glass. "I already told you. Cold feet. I'm sure you'll find a way to warm her up once we find her."

Paul had at least a million reasons to try, thanks to Rupert Casville's incentive program. The old man had agreed to deposit a million dollars in Paul's bank account as soon as he and Mimi were married. Paul would receive another million if Rupert's first grandchild was conceived within a year, as well as a hefty share of Casville Industries stock.

The telephone rang, startling them both. Rupert shot out of his chair. "I'll bet this is it."

Paul watched Rupert pick up the receiver, then saw his expectant expression fade as he rubbed one hand over the gray stubble on his face. Try as he might, Paul was unable to make out the low mumblings of the phone conversation.

His gaze moved to the silver flask of vodka on the table. His biggest weakness. If he could give up alcohol, he could do anything. Now was not the time to lose control. Mimi's escape didn't have to mean the end of his dreams. Just a temporary delay.

Rupert heaved a long sigh as he hung up the telephone receiver. "That was Harper. He's checked the airport, train station and bus terminal, but no sign of Mimi. As far as he can tell, she's still somewhere in Austin."

"Unless she left the city in her car."

Rupert shook his head. "Her car wouldn't get her very far since she left her wallet and credit cards at home. She brought that silly little white purse with her to the church, and it barely had enough room for her car keys and driver's license."

Paul tensed. "So where is she?"

"Hell if I know," Rupert snapped, raking his hand through his thinning gray hair. Then he looked up, worry lines etched in his brow. "Do you think she's all right?"

Paul thought she was a spoiled princess who needed a good spanking, but he knew better than to say it out loud. "I'm sure she's fine. Mimi knows how to take care of herself. She'll be home before you know it, safe and sound."

"I hope so." Rupert sighed. "I'm exhausted. I stayed up half the night waiting for her to come home."

No doubt the vodka was kicking in, too. Paul picked up the flask and handed it to him. "Go get some sleep. I'll stay here and handle any incoming business calls."

Rupert slipped the flask into his pocket. "Wake me if you hear anything new from Harper."

"I will." Paul placed his hand on the old man's shoulder as they walked toward the door. "And don't worry. I'll take care of everything."

GARRETT OPENED his eyes, squinting at the sunshine streaming through his bedroom window—a sign that it was long past daybreak. Surprised that he'd overslept, he threw back the covers and sat up in bed. Something niggled at the back of his sleep-numbed brain. Something important. He yawned, stretching his arms over his head.

Then he smelled bacon frying.

Mimi. The peace of the morning shattered as reality came rushing back. She was the reason he'd tossed and turned most of the night, snatches of erotic dreams invading his sleep. Dreams she'd invoked with her lilting voice and her inviting mouth and those incredible eyes.

Garrett rubbed one hand over the rough whiskers on his face, trying to remember just how long it had been since he'd slept with a woman. Finding female companionship had never been a problem, but lately he'd been too wrapped up searching for his birth mother to make time for anything else.

Garrett stood up as the aroma of fresh-brewed coffee teased his nostrils. He dressed and shaved at twice the usual speed, driven by the gnawing hunger in his stomach and the need to apologize to Mimi for his temper last night. The shock of finding a runaway bride hiding in his hayloft was no excuse. The least he could do was offer to give her a ride to her car first thing this morning and fill the tank with gas.

"Good morning," she said cheerfully as he walked into the kitchen. She stood at the stove wearing one of his old flannel shirts, the tails hanging almost to her knees. The denim jeans she wore looked suspiciously familiar, too, the long legs rolled at the ankles. Her feet were bare, and her silky blond hair hung loose around her shoulders.

He shifted from one boot to the other, his throat suddenly dry and his heart pounding double-time. The stylish bride from the night before had disappeared. In her place was a woman who looked as if she'd just rolled out of his bed, her hair tousled and a sexy flush on her cheeks.

She transferred the bacon strips from the frying pan onto a plate, then flashed him a smile. "I found these clothes in your laundry room. I hope you don't mind."

He swallowed hard. "Not at all. Did you sleep well?"

Her smile widened. "I haven't slept so well in years. It's so quiet and peaceful out here. If you could bottle up the serenity and sell it, you'd make millions."

Serene wasn't exactly the way he felt when he looked at her.

"I hope you're hungry," she said, setting the bacon on the table next to a colorful egg casserole and a pot of steaming coffee.

"Starving," he said, pulling out a chair for her and telling himself to confine his appetite to breakfast.

She served a hearty portion of the casserole on his plate, then watched expectantly as he forked up his first bite. "Well?"

He let the succulent flavors linger on his tongue, then swallowed. "What is it?"

"A vegetable frittata."

He scooped up another bite. "What kind of vegetables?"

She picked up her coffee cup. "Onions and tomatoes and broccoli. Among other things."

He reached for the serving spoon and covered half his plate with more of the frittata. "If you can make broccoli taste this good, you're the one who will make millions."

She laughed, and his heartbeat kicked up another notch. He picked up his coffee cup, telling himself it was a good thing she'd be gone soon or he could be in big trouble.

"Oh, I almost forgot," she said, setting down her fork. "You got a phone call while you were in the shower. Some woman from the employment agency had a question about the position you want filled."

Garrett swallowed a sigh of irritation. He'd contacted the agency over two weeks ago looking for a temporary employee. At this rate, calving season would be over before he ever got a ranch hand hired. "Did she leave a number?"

"No."

He looked up from his plate. "Is she planning to call me back later?"

Mimi tucked a stray curl behind her ear. "No, but she is refunding your money."

He scowled. "Why?"

"Because I told her the position is already filled."

His stomach lurched, unsettling the large amount of vegetable frittata he'd just inhaled. Garrett wasn't psychic, but he did have good instincts. And those instincts were telling him that trouble had already arrived. He took a deep breath, determined to remain calm. "Do you mind telling me why you did that?"

"You don't need to find a ranch hand," Mimi said, opening her arms wide. "You're looking at her."

Apprehension skittered across his spine. "Absolutely not."

She leaned forward. "But, Garrett, I know I can do it. And this way you don't have to waste time and money advertising for a ranch hand. I'm willing to work hard from sunup to sundown. And even longer, if necessary."

His gaze fell to her chest, his whole body tightening at the way she filled out his old flannel work shirt. If he couldn't even eat eggs with Mimi without fantasizing about her, how could he possibly work with her?

"Forget it," he finally said. "You're not cut out for ranch life. You'll be much happier back in the city where you belong." He stood up. "Thanks for breakfast. I'm going to feed the horses, which should give you just enough time to get cleaned up and ready to go."

"Where exactly am I going?"

"That's totally up to you. I'll take you as far as your car." His resolve wavered a little when he saw the bleak disappointment on her face. "Surely you have friends or family, someone who can help you."

She shook her head. "I can't go back to Austin."

"Can't or won't?"

She didn't say anything, just stared mutely at the coffee cup in her hands.

For the second time he wondered if she was in danger. He'd given refuge to a woman in danger before. And paid the price. He absently rubbed his left shoulder. The bullet hadn't done any serious damage. The wound was scarred over, but still a little tender.

Of course, that had been an unusual situation. Jake Maitland had asked him to give Camille Eckart and her baby a place to hide from her abusive ex-husband. The old cabin on the outskirts of his ranch had provided the perfect sanctuary for them. At least, until Camille's ex-husband showed up, armed and definitely dangerous. He'd tried to kill her, but had ended up dead by the time the confrontation was over. Garrett had suffered the only injury, but it still chilled him to think of the harm that might have come to Camille or her baby.

Still, Mimi didn't act like a woman in jeopardy. She didn't have the same shadow of fear that had hovered around Camille. No, Mimi was probably just afraid to face her fiancé. Or her family, who no doubt had gone into debt to pay for her fancy wedding. Still, what would it hurt him to grant her a temporary refuge?

Garrett firmed his jaw, feeling himself weakening. He couldn't solve Mimi's problems. He had enough of his own to handle.

"Do you need money?" he asked, trying to assuage his pesky conscience.

She met his gaze and tipped up her chin. "I don't take charity. I'm willing to work for room and board, Garrett. The lady from the employment agency read the job requirements over the phone to me. It's just a temporary job, which is exactly what I need. Just a month to get my life straightened out."

A month. He'd barely made it through one night. The thought of having Mimi around day after day, night after night was enough to make him break into a sweat.

He shook his head. "You don't understand. This is a working ranch. I raise registered Texas longhorns. I've got customers coming out all the time to buy breeding stock, so I need a ranch hand who can pick up the slack when I'm busy making a sale. Usually I can handle it on my own, but I do need help to get through calving season. *Experienced* help."

"I'm a fast learner," she countered.

He arched a brow. "Can you fix fence? Pull a calf? Brand? Vaccinate? Ride a horse?"

His litany of chores didn't daunt her. "I can ride a horse and I'm willing to learn the rest."

He reached for the doorknob. "Maybe so, but I don't have time to teach you."

"Garrett," she began, "wait..."

But he walked out the door before she could say another word. Relief washed over him with every step that put distance between him and Mimi. He'd been too close to accepting her offer and letting her stay.

Much too close.

CHAPTER THREE

MIMI HAD NEVER believed in miracles.

Until Garrett turned his pickup truck onto the country road where she'd left her convertible yesterday. The *empty* country road.

"Are you sure this is the place?" he asked, slowing the truck to a snail's pace.

"Positive." She pointed out the front windshield. "I recognize that mesquite tree."

"So where is your car?"

"Someone must have stolen it." She tried to sound forlorn, but it was hard when her prospects were suddenly looking so much better.

He snorted. "This area is hardly a hotbed for car thieves." He braked to a stop, then cut the engine. "It's got to be around here somewhere. A car just can't disappear."

Mimi climbed out of the truck and joined him in the middle of the road, telling herself not to get her hopes up. He could still refuse to hire her.

He stood with his hands on his lean hips and a disgruntled expression on his face. "What have I done to deserve this?"

She looked at him, squinting in the glare of the morning sun. "Maybe it's a sign."

"I don't believe in signs." He stalked to the truck. "I'll just take you back to Austin myself."

"Okay," she said, trudging along beside him. "You can drop me off on a street corner somewhere."

He stopped to frown at her. "I don't think so."

"A homeless shelter?"

A muscle flexed in his square jaw. "Stop fooling around, Mimi. Tell me your address."

She folded her arms across her chest. "I assure you I'm completely serious. You may not want me to work for you, but you can't force me to go home, either."

He narrowed his eyes. "You're trying to make me feel guilty. It won't work."

"I'm not trying to make you feel anything. I'm just telling you I won't go home. Not yet."

"Then when?"

She gave a slight shrug. "Maybe in about four weeks."

He looked at the sky, but she couldn't tell if he was contemplating hiring her or leaving her out here to the coyotes. Suddenly, she wanted more than a refuge from her problems. She wanted to get to know Garrett and his life out here. A life that was so different from her own.

Mimi heard him swear softly under his breath before he turned to face her. "You're serious, aren't you? You really want to hire on as my ranch hand?"

Her heart leaped. "I've always wanted to work outdoors."

He shook his head. "Ranching isn't some glamour job. And it's nothing like what you've seen on television. It's hard, dirty, exhausting work."

"I'm not afraid of hard work."

"How about ice storms? This January is looking to be worse than usual. And we work every day, rain or shine. I mean every day, no weekends or holidays off. During calving season, we take shifts and work through the night, too."

"You're trying to scare me. It won't work."

"I'm just telling you the facts of ranching life. You'll get kicked by cows, stung by bees and definitely break every single one of those fancy fingernails. Ranching is tough for any woman. But for a city woman, it's downright impossible."

She arched a brow. "You have a pretty low opinion of me, don't you, Garrett?"

He sighed. "It's nothing personal. I just don't have time to waste coddling a tenderfoot. This is a working ranch, not some vacation spot for bored debutantes."

His words stung. "I'm not looking for a vacation. I expect to earn my keep. I'm just grateful you're willing to give me a chance."

He opened his mouth, then closed it again. "Wait just a minute," he began. "When did I offer to give you a chance?"

"Are you a gambling man, Garrett?"

He folded his arms across his chest. "Only when the odds are in my favor."

She moved a step closer to him, the air crackling between them. Yesterday she'd blamed her initial attraction to him on exhaustion and nerves. But today she was drawn to him even more. His strength and vitality appealed to something primal inside her. Something that made her want to throw off the stuffy constraints of her upbringing and make him really see her. Make him believe she was a woman worthy of his respect.

She looked at him. "Let's make a little wager. I'll work here for three days. If I can keep up—"

"And keep out of trouble," he interjected.

"Then you'll let me stay."

"But if you can't keep up, then you'll give me your address and let me take you home. Deal?"

Three days. She just hoped it was long enough to prove herself to him. Still, it wasn't as if she had any options. "Deal."

He smiled, obviously convinced he'd gotten the best of her. "Don't expect me to go easy on you just because you're a woman. I'll treat you like I'd treat any other ranch hand."

She resisted the urge to do a little victory dance right in the middle of the road. "Absolutely. I wouldn't have it any other way."

"And don't be afraid to tell me when you've had enough. I can take you back at any time. You don't have to stick it out for the whole three days."

He was very confident. Alarmingly so. For one brief moment, Mimi wondered what exactly she'd gotten herself into. Then she shook off her qualms. Nothing could be as bad as facing her father and Paul.

Their betrayal still cut into her like a knife. A shiver ran through her when she realized how close she'd come to marrying Paul. Especially when her short time with Garrett had elicited a more intense physical reaction than she'd ever experienced with her fiancé.

"Second thoughts?" he asked, misinterpreting her silence.

"Not at all," she replied, squaring her shoulders. "What do you want me to do first?"

He tipped up his cowboy hat. "Well, for starters, you could tell me your full name."

"Banyon." She improvised with only a moment's hesitation. Her mother's maiden name wasn't nearly as recognizable as Casville. It also wasn't in the Austin phone directory, just in case this was a trick and he planned to call every Banyon in Austin until he found one who would claim her.

She tilted her head at him. "And yours?"

"The name's Lord. Garrett Lord."

She held out her hand. "It's a pleasure to be working for you, Mr. Lord."

He clasped her hand in his, and Mimi couldn't ignore the warm tingle that shot up her arm. Then he smiled and said, "I think you're in for a surprise, Miss Banyon."

"Just remember, I get three days."

His smile widened. "Mimi, you won't even last one day."

SHE BARELY LASTED one hour.

First, she stepped into a gopher hole, wrenched her ankle and landed in a fresh pile of cow manure. It only got worse after that. By dusk, her entire body ached from the arduous task of helping Garrett fix fence. It didn't sound difficult, but it took muscle power to straighten fence posts and tighten barbed wire. Unfortunately, her one-day-a-week workouts at Austin's trendiest fitness center hadn't prepared her for life on the range.

"Ouch!" Mimi gasped as a razor-sharp barb on the wire fencing pricked her finger.

"There's a pair of leather gloves in the truck cab," Garrett informed her as he tightened the barbed wire with the wire stretchers.

"I'm fine," she replied, feeling a little woozy as she watched blood ooze out of her thumb. She closed her eyes and hastily wiped her thumb on her jeans. No doubt it blended in well with the dirt and manure already staining them. If Garrett wasn't yet having second thoughts about giving her free access to the clothes his sister Shelby had left here, he soon would be.

She was filthy from head to toe. He, on the other hand, looked wonderful. His faded blue denim jeans outlined his powerful legs and trim backside. Perspiration molded his white cotton shirt to his broad chest, delineating every well-defined muscle. The only dirt he'd collected was a fine layer of dust on his scuffed cowboy boots and a tiny smudge of mud on the side of his jaw.

She was staring again. When he looked up and caught her gaze, something hot and sweet uncoiled inside her. She liked his mouth and found herself wondering how it would feel against hers. If he kissed her, the dark whiskers shading his jaw would scrape against her skin. She swallowed at the imagined sensation.

"How about some water?" he asked, his voice slightly husky.

She nodded, not trusting herself to speak. When he brought her the jug, she took a long drink of the icy water.

"The sun's hot today," he said, removing his cowboy hat and wiping his forearm over his brow.

Not quite as hot as her employer, Mimi thought, handing over the jug. Then she turned her attention to the fence, where she inadvertently snagged her thumb on another razor-sharp barb. "Ouch!"

Garrett lowered the jug from his mouth, moisture glistening on his lower lip. "Our deal didn't include you acting like a martyr. Go put those gloves on."

"Don't worry about me, Garrett." She looked away from him, wiping her thumb on the back of her jeans. From now on she needed to pay more attention to her work and less to her boss. "I may be a city girl, but I'm tougher than I look."

He shook his head, then surveyed the length of fence. "Looks as if we're done here for today, anyway."

With an inward sigh of relief, Mimi walked toward the pickup truck, trying her best not to limp. She climbed into the cab, every joint in her body protesting the movement. All she wanted now was a long, hot bubble bath, followed by a warm, soft bed.

Garrett opened the driver's door, and Hubert jumped in ahead of him. The little dog pranced across the bench seat, then lay down with his head on Mimi's thigh.

She lightly petted the dog with her sore fingers. "Where did you find Hubert?"

"Actually, he found me," Garrett said as the pickup roared to life. "Someone decided they didn't want him anymore and dumped him off in the country. He was skinny as a hickory stick by the time he finally wandered onto the ranch."

"But he's such a sweet dog. I can't believe anyone would dump him on purpose."

"Believe it," he said. "Some people seem to labor under the stupid illusion that just because he's an animal, a dog can survive in the wild. They don't realize that he's never learned to hunt for food and water. Or that there are predators out here, like coyotes, just waiting for an easy kill."

"So you saved him?"

Garrett kept his eyes on the gravel road. "I fed him, and he decided to stick around. He's not the best cow dog in Texas, but he tries hard."

Hubert closed his eyes in canine bliss as Mimi scratched behind his ears. "How did you ever come up with the name Hubert?"

"That was the name on his fancy rhinestone collar. When he showed up on my doorstep, he still had it on, along with a frayed pink bow and pink toenails."

"I still can't believe someone could just dump him, then take off." She shook her head. "How could anyone be so cruel?"

A muscle twitched in Garrett's jaw. "Happens all the time. And not just to animals."

Before she could ask him to explain, a loud horn sounded behind them.

"Damn."

"What's the problem?"

"It's not a what, it's a who." He steered the pickup truck to the edge of the road, then rolled down his window as another pickup pulled up beside them.

The petite brunette in the driver's seat smiled at him. "Hey, Garrett. I see you've got a tagalong today."

"Venna Schwab, this is Mimi Banyon. She just hired on for calving season."

Mimi was surprised to hear him sound so cheerful about it. Especially since he'd been silent and surly most of the afternoon.

Venna rested her elbow on the truck door, her gaze flicking over Mimi. "Really?"

Mimi leaned forward in the seat and waved. "Nice to meet you."

Venna wrinkled her nose. "You're a mess, honey."

Mimi forced a smile. "Nothing a little hot water can't cure."

Venna shrugged, then turned her attention to Garrett. "I hope having an extra hand around means you won't have to work so hard. I've hardly seen you lately."

"It's almost calving season, Venna. You're probably as busy as I am at the Triple C."

She laughed. "True. But I can always make time for a little fun."

Mimi definitely felt like a third wheel. She thought about hopping out of the cab and walking the rest of the way to the house, just barely visible in the distance, but her aching body protested that idea.

Venna leaned a little further out the window. "Speaking of fun, are you going to Connor and Lacy O'Hara's barbecue on Saturday night?"

Garrett nodded. "I planned on it."

"Good. Do you need a date?"

Mimi wondered when she'd become invisible. Venna sure wasn't letting the presence of Garrett's hired help put a damper on her outrageous flirting.

"Actually, I'm taking Mimi to the barbecue."

"You are?" Mimi exclaimed, realizing a second too late that it was the wrong thing to say.

Garrett turned to her. "Yes. I am."

"Oh."

Venna looked between the two of them, confusion wrinkling her brow. "You're taking your ranch hand on a date?"

Garrett cleared his throat. "I wouldn't exactly call it a date."

"What would you call it?" Venna asked, her gaze fixed on Mimi. Perhaps she finally saw some competition behind all the dirt and manure.

Mimi leaned forward. "I'm sure Garrett's just being polite. I might not even be here on Saturday, so he may be free after all."

"Thanks a lot," Garrett growled under his breath.

"I'll be sure and give you a call, Garrett." Venna waved as she drove away, leaving a cloud of dust lingering in the hazy twilight.

"She seems nice," Mimi said as Garrett pulled the pickup onto the road.

"Nice enough."

"Pretty, too."

He glanced at her. "Pretty enough to snag two husbands."

She waited for him to elaborate, but he kept his gaze focused on the road. She'd heard about the strong, silent type, but this was ridiculous. At least now she understood why he was avoiding Venna. She tried to ignore the tiny glimmer of satisfaction it gave her. Garrett's love life, or lack of one, shouldn't matter to her one bit.

Leaning back against seat, she gazed at the sun

hovering on the horizon, awed by the beautiful palette of colors arcing across the sky. Was there any place more beautiful than this?

Garrett pulled the pickup truck into the driveway, then cut the engine. "We need to talk."

Now, there was a novel idea. "What about?"

"About where you're going to sleep tonight."

"Oh. I forgot about that." Her cheeks warmed as she realized she'd just taken for granted that he'd invite her to stay at the house. Did a ranch hand normally sleep in the barn? She'd enjoyed her brief interlude in the hayloft yesterday, but she wasn't sure she wanted to sleep there for the next four weeks. Especially if it was occupied by mice, rats or other assorted rodents.

"I've been remodeling the second floor, so the bedrooms up there are a mess. I used to have a small cabin on my ranch that was used for a bunkhouse, but it burned down last month."

"So that leaves?"

"My bed."

"Your bed?" she echoed, certain she hadn't heard him right.

He gazed at her through half-lidded eyes. "I think you'll find my bed much more comfortable than my sofa."

Maybe. But she doubted she'd get any sleep in his bed. For one brief moment, she allowed herself to imagine sleeping in Garrett Lord's bed. In his arms. Kissing that hard, sullen mouth. A bolt of white-hot desire shot through her veins.

She closed her eyes, telling herself she shouldn't be having erotic thoughts about another man already.

"I think I prefer the sofa," she said at last.

"Sorry, that's not an option."

At the unyielding tone of his voice, her mouth fell open. Was this how he planned to get rid of her? Then she looked into Garrett's green-gold eyes and knew she was overreacting. This wasn't a man who played games. "Why not?"

"Because I'll be sleeping on the sofa. It's roomy, but not quite big enough for two."

She shook her head. "I can't kick you out of your own bed."

He shrugged, then opened the door and climbed out of the pickup. "It will only be for a night or two."

Her regret burned away at the arrogant confidence in his tone. *The big jerk.* Garrett Lord thought he'd be rid of her soon. Thought she was a spoiled city girl who would run back to Austin the first time she broke a nail.

She didn't want to admit to herself that the thought of returning to Austin had crossed her mind a time or two in the last few hours. But Garrett's doubts about her staying power strengthened her resolve.

"A night or two?" she muttered, following Garrett to the house and trying not to wince every painful step of the way. "Think again, cowboy."

"Did you say something?" he asked as he held the door open for her.

"I said thanks for giving up your bed." She smiled sweetly at him. "I'll take it."

GARRETT STRETCHED on the sofa and silently counted the chimes of the grandfather clock. Nine...ten... eleven...twelve. Midnight. He'd been lying here wide awake for almost two hours and wondering where he'd gone wrong. He had a beautiful woman in his bed. And he was on the sofa. Somehow, some way, he'd screwed up.

He bunched the pillow under his head and turned onto his side, the lonestar quilt slipping off his shoulder. Hubert slept soundly on the rug in front of the fireplace. No doubt Mimi slept soundly, too, after the day she'd put in. Hell, she'd dozed off over supper. He smiled into the darkness, remembering how he'd moved her plate away just in time to keep her hair from falling into the ketchup.

Then his smile faded. He was thinking about her too much. Way too damn much. She'd be gone in a day or two. Besides, she had a fiancé waiting for her out there somewhere.

Just like he had a mother out there somewhere. Only she wasn't waiting for him or his brother or sisters to find her. In fact, she'd made it almost impossible. How could one woman disappear so easily? *LeeAnn Larrimore.* A name as unfamiliar to him as the woman he'd once called Mama.

The search for her had finally narrowed down to the last name on the list. A list that had started with the names of women who had given birth to fraternal triplets in Texas around the same time period and with the right sex: two girls, one boy. One by one, the other names on the list had been eliminated as possibilities. So had any other potential leads. That left only LeeAnn Larrimore.

According to his research, she'd given birth to triplets at a free clinic in a town near Austin. She'd lived in Austin for a while, working in a grocery store until she'd been fired from her job. That's when the trail had turned ice cold.

He flipped onto his stomach and closed his eyes, willing sleep to overtake him. He didn't want to think about the woman who had abandoned her children twenty-five years ago. And he definitely didn't want to think about the woman sleeping in his bed. How her silky blond curls would spill over the pillow. Or the way her body would warm the white cotton sheets, imbuing them with her unique scent. He closed his eyes, imagining the soft, steady cadence of her breathing as she slept. Then he imagined waking her with a kiss. Sliding his hands under the sheets and touching her. Making her breathing quicken.

"Garrett?" Mimi's soft voice trickled over him in the darkness.

His eyes shot open, his heart beating wildly in his chest. He took a moment to steady his breathing, then cleared his throat. "What?"

She stepped into the living room. "Are you awake?"

"Yes." He sat up, the quilt falling down around his hips. He shifted it slightly to hide the evidence of his desire. Then he saw her gaze drift to his bare chest and linger there.

"Did you want something?" he asked, his voice sounding rougher than he'd intended. Of course, Mimi didn't help matters by looking so damn delectable. The woman had invaded not only his barn and his house and his bed, but his closet, as well. She wore an old T-shirt of his for a nightgown, the hem barely reaching mid-thigh. It revealed her long, slender legs, and he caught the faint scent of apples as she walked into the living room. She'd taken a bubble bath before supper and obviously found his sister's stash of scented bath products.

Garrett's breath caught as she moved closer to him, her blond hair gleaming in the soft glow of the fire. The shadows dancing in the room made it impossible to see her expression or read anything in her beautiful blue eyes. Was she purposely trying to torture him?

Or seduce him?

His fingers curled around the quilt at that thought. Part of him wanted to deny that Mimi would use her body as a ticket to stay on at his ranch. Another part of him desperately wanted it to be true. He swallowed hard. "What do you need?"

"I thought I heard something."

He arched a brow, wondering whether to believe her. Some women played the damsel-in-distress part to the hilt, although Mimi hadn't struck him as the deceptive type. Still, look at her track record. She'd stowed away in his hayloft. Stood up her fiancé at the altar. Found a way to sweet-talk him into offering her a job as a ranch hand—even if it was just on a trial basis.

She tensed, then looked toward the large bay window. "There it is again." She lowered her voice to almost a whisper. "Do you hear it?"

"Turn around."

She blinked. "Why?"

He sat up and swung his legs over the side of the sofa. "You can either turn around or you can watch me put my pants on."

She whirled. Garrett grabbed his jeans, grateful for the darkness that would cover the evidence of his arousal. Now he just needed to cover her. He picked up the quilt and tossed it to her. "Here, you're going to need this. Come with me."

Without a word, she wrapped the quilt around her shoulders, effectively concealing all that silky bare skin, then followed Garrett out the front door.

He stood at the railing of his front porch, feeling the grooves of the smoothly worn slat flooring under his bare feet. The air was cool and crisp, with endless stars twinkling in the night sky. The moon cast a gentle glow over the rolling hills and crags of the land he loved so much.

In the distance, the sound of high-pitched yipping carried across the peaceful night. "Is that the sound you heard?"

She moved beside him, pulling the quilt more tightly around her shoulders. "Yes."

"It's coyotes. Haven't you ever heard them before?"

She unconsciously moved another step closer to him. "Sure. In the movies. But I thought they howled."

He smelled apples and something else. Something uniquely Mimi. "They do sometimes. This sounds like a pack with pups. The full moon can make them crazy. Or maybe they just made a kill."

"A kill?"

"A jackrabbit or maybe a possum." He frowned into the darkness. "Sounds like they're in the south pasture."

She looked at him, the moonlight illuminating the concern on her face. "Maybe they killed one of the cows."

He shook his head. ''They're smart enough not to go up against a twelve-hundred-pound cow with sharp horns. But a calf is another story.''

''Can't the mother cow protect it?''

''Not always. Coyotes work in groups. Half of them will distract a mama cow while the rest of them bring down the calf. She'll put up a hell of a fight to protect her baby, though. And she'll bawl for days afterward if she loses it.''

''That's awful. Can't you do anything to protect them?''

''A good dog will keep coyotes at bay.''

''Like Hubert?''

He laughed. ''Hubert? The coyotes would think he was a tasty midnight snack, not a threat. That's why I let him sleep in the house.''

''Seems like you've made a habit of taking in strays.'' Mimi rested one hand on the porch railing, gazing into the night. ''You're a nice man, Garrett Lord.''

He looked at her, wondering what she'd say if she knew he was thinking some not-so-nice thoughts right now. About her. About how he'd like to strip off that quilt and that old shirt and make love to her under the stars.

Mimi made the mistake of turning to him at that moment, her face tilted to ask him another question. He didn't give her a chance. He captured her mouth with his, savoring her sweet soft lips as his hands rested lightly on her shoulders.

He closed his eyes as he breathed in her scent and sought refuge in the warm sanctuary of her mouth. She didn't move at first, then her hands slid slowly up his bare chest. He deepened the kiss, her touch drawing a low moan from within his chest.

A shrill bark brought him to his senses. He abruptly stepped away from her, then looked at the porch floor to see Hubert sitting between their feet, wagging his tail.

Garrett took another step away from Mimi, letting the night breeze cool his overheated body. She was an engaged woman—reason enough to keep his distance—and vulnerable. He knew how badly she wanted to stay here. It would be unfair to take advantage of that fact. "Looks like the moon is making everybody crazy tonight. Sorry."

"Garrett, I…"

"Forget it," he said, not giving her a chance to comment on that kiss. He didn't want to talk about it. He didn't even want to think about it. When she didn't move, he met her gaze and saw his hunger reflected in her eyes. Or was that wishful thinking on his part? "You should go back to bed."

She hesitated, then without another word, she walked into the house and closed the door behind her. If he was lucky, that kiss would scare her off, and he'd wake up to find her gone in the morning.

But Garrett was never lucky. He'd always had to work for whatever he wanted. Now he just had to decide if he wanted Mimi to go.

Or stay.

CHAPTER FOUR

A LOUD POUNDING woke Mimi from a sound sleep, then the bedroom door opened a crack. "Time to get up. We're wasting daylight."

She rubbed her eyes, then looked toward the window into the pitch-black darkness beyond. Even the sun knew it was too early to be up yet.

"Five more minutes," she said groggily, flopping onto the pillow.

Garrett called through the open door. "You can sleep until noon if you want, Mimi. Then I'll take you back to Austin after lunch."

His words were more effective than a bucket of ice-cold spring water. "All right, all right," she said with a groan. "I'm up."

She rose to her feet, every aching joint screaming in protest. Wincing, she moved to the dresser and stared into the mirror. Unfortunately, she looked even worse than she felt. Her face was red with sunburn, her nose was peeling and her hair stuck out at odd angles.

She'd seen Garrett's reflection in the mirror when he woke her. He'd looked as handsome as ever in his old jeans and worn chambray shirt. He'd tasted wonderful, too. She closed her eyes for a moment, reliving that kiss.

With a sigh, she reached for the hairbrush on top of the dresser. Still only half-awake, she knocked her hand against the small, tattered teddy bear perched on the corner of the dresser, sending it to the floor. She bent to pick it up, aware of the ominous creaking in her sore knees.

It was old. Very old. With black button eyes and an odd stitching pattern on the mouth that gave it a whimsical smile. The excelsior stuffing had shifted inside it, making it too thin in some places and too thick in others.

Mimi carefully replaced the teddy bear on the dresser, letting her fingers caress the worn brown fur on its belly. She'd been too exhausted last night to notice the bear, but now she realized how incongruously it stood out in the utilitarian bedroom. Garrett didn't have any pictures on the walls or other knick-knacks. Just a bed, a dresser, a desk and a teddy bear.

Mimi smiled as she ran the brush through her tangled tresses. Garrett Lord didn't seem like the teddy bear type. But then, what did she really know about the man, other than that he was a hell of a good kisser. She worked her hair into a neat braid, then secured the ends with a ponytail holder. She shouldn't have let him kiss her last night.

She shouldn't have *wanted* him to kiss her.

Her life was already complicated enough without adding romance into the mix. Besides, she wanted to prove to Garrett that she could work as well as any ranch hand. And somehow she doubted kissing was included in the job description. She wanted him to let her stay because she deserved it, not because he was attracted to her.

But despite her logical thinking, a tingle of excitement rippled through her. Not only had Garrett kissed her, he'd kissed her not knowing she was heir to the Casville fortune. He'd wanted Mimi for herself, not for her money or the power the Casville name could yield.

But the heady feeling faded when she sat down to put on Shelby's cowboy boots. Her feet were swollen and still very sore from her barefoot trek down the gravel road, making the boots almost impossible to pull on.

"Mimi?" Garrett's shout carried down the hallway. "Let's go!"

Gritting her teeth, she tugged hard, finally pulling on the right boot. Swallowing a sob of pain, she reached for the left boot. She could do this. She *had* to do this—to prove to Garrett she wasn't some spoiled city girl. And to prove it to herself.

By the time she reached the kitchen, her feet had molded themselves to the leather boots, and the pain had receded a little. She took a deep breath and squared her shoulders, ready to face another day on the range. "Sorry I took so long."

"I made us some fried-egg sandwiches and coffee to take with us." Garrett grabbed two paper bags off the counter, along with two small thermoses. "We can eat on the way."

"Where are we going?"

"To the north pasture. I'd like to move the cows closer to the barn before they start calving. Oh, and grab one of those yellow slickers from the mud porch. It looks like rain."

Mimi followed him out the back door, slipping the

slicker over her head. Hubert ran along beside her, barking shrilly and nipping at her heels. Then he spun in circles, chasing his tail, obviously excited to start the day.

She looked at the ominous black clouds filling the sky and heard a low rumble of thunder in the distance. Garrett had told her to expect to work rain or shine, so she kept her mouth shut as she followed him to the truck. Except this morning he walked right past the truck and headed for the barn. Mimi quickened her pace to catch up with his long strides.

The sweet smell of hay mingled with the earthy scent of horses when he opened the barn door. "I've saddled up Pooh for you," he said, motioning toward a far stall. "He shouldn't give you any problems."

Mimi smiled. "Pooh?"

"Shelby named him." Garrett stuffed his thermos and breakfast sack into a saddlebag. "Let's go."

Mimi led the dappled gelding out of the barn just as a light, icy drizzle began to fall. She patted Pooh's velvety nose, thankful that her father had insisted on riding lessons when she was eight. Horseback riding was the one activity on this ranch she knew she could handle.

Until it started to rain.

Mimi had done most of her riding in an enclosed arena. She wasn't used to having the wind whip rain into her face or maneuvering around mud puddles. Thankfully, the slicker kept most of her body dry, and the hot coffee kept her warm.

"How much farther?" she called to Garrett, who was one horse length ahead of her.

"Only another mile," he yelled over the rumble of thunder above them.

She took the last bite of her cold, soggy egg sandwich, then reached down to pat the neck of her horse. Poor Pooh was trudging through mud up to his fetlocks. Mimi wished she'd thought to bring along a pocketful of sugar cubes to reward him.

At last they reached the north pasture, where twenty wet and obviously pregnant Texas longhorn cows stood unmoving as the horses approached. They didn't look happy, and Mimi didn't blame them one bit.

Garrett climbed off his horse and swung open the wide gate. Then he walked over to her, rainwater running off his cowboy hat as he looked at her on her horse. "We'll herd them along that shallow ravine until we reach the corral just east of the barn."

Herd them? She glanced at the truculent cows, then at Garrett. "What if they don't want to go?"

"Then we'll be out here in the rain a hell of a long time," he said, trudging to his horse. He climbed on, then trotted into the pasture.

Mimi followed, wishing he'd provided a few more details. Exactly how did one herd cattle? Was she supposed to yell at them? Wave her arms in the air? Give them a map?

She watched Garrett ride his horse along the perimeter of the herd, and she did the same on the opposite side. The cows slowly lumbered toward the gate. Garrett and Mimi gradually contracted the perimeter until the cows were in a tight group. The herd began to head through the open gate, rain still falling from the sky and soaking into their thick hides.

Mimi was just congratulating herself on how easy this herding business was when one of the cows balked and turned right in front of her, galloping back into the pasture. She looked frantically at Garrett, who was busy keeping the cattle moving through the gate and hadn't noticed the escape. She opened her mouth to call for help, then closed it again. Somehow she knew a real ranch hand wouldn't run to the boss each time something went wrong. Besides, it was just one cow. How hard could it be to bring her back to the herd?

She tugged on Pooh's reins, wheeling the horse around and galloping into the pasture after the stray cow. The animal stared at her for a long moment with soulful brown eyes. Rainwater glistened on the long, sharp horns. Then the cow turned and bolted into the ravine.

Mimi glanced over her shoulder at Garrett. He sat on his horse watching her as the rest of the cattle moved meekly through the gate. She lifted her arm and waved to him. "Go on," she shouted. "I'll catch up with you."

He hesitated, then waved to her before following the rest of the herd.

She turned her attention to the recalcitrant cow. "All right, I know it probably isn't any fun to have to move to a new place in the rain, but you really don't have any choice in the matter."

The cow ignored her, lowering its head to tug on a wilted weed. Mimi edged her horse closer, hoping she didn't spook the cow. It turned and looked at her, contentedly chewing on the weed, half of it sticking out of its mouth.

"Look, I know I'm new at this," she said, gently nudging Pooh's flanks to move the horse even closer. Pooh tossed his head in the air to protest the idea, but Mimi remained firm. "But I'm trying to make a good impression on Garrett. He'll kick my butt back to Austin if I can't do a simple job like herding."

The cow kept chewing, seemingly unmoved by Mimi's plight. Thunder rumbled in the sky, and a gust of wind blew the hood of the slicker off her head. She reached to grab it as rain plastered her hair over her eyes.

At that moment, the cow decided Pooh was too close, and she lowered her head and charged. Pooh reared on his hind legs, and Mimi, her hands on the slicker hood instead of the reins, slid backward off the saddle, over Pooh's broad rump and onto the soggy ground.

She sat there, stunned for a moment. Then she wiped the rain and splattered mud off her face just in time to see Pooh lurch forward and take off at a fast gallop toward the far end of the pasture. The cow stood her ground, eyeing Mimi distrustfully.

Mimi took one look at those sharp, lethal horns and scooted backward in the mud. "Nice cow."

The cow took a step toward her.

"Go away, nice cow. I'm not going to hurt you."

The cow took another step.

She glanced frantically over her shoulder, but Garrett and the rest of the herd were out of sight. Pooh was keeping his distance, too, and had turned his attention to grazing. Mimi swallowed hard as she turned to face the cow. Cold, wet mud had soaked through her jeans, and the jarring fall had given her one hell of a headache.

So much for her expensive riding-academy lessons.

As she continued to scoot backward, her hand closed over a hard, flattened dirt clod. She picked it up and hurled it at the cow. The clod bounced off the cow's nose, making the animal snort and jump backward. Tasting success, Mimi picked up another clod and aimed for the same spot. The cow backed, turning away from Mimi. But Mimi wasn't about to give up. She got to her feet and began gathering the flattened clods that lay scattered over the pasture.

"Let's go," she cried to the cow, hurling a clod at the hind end. The cow bolted out of the ravine and began heading in the direction of the gate.

Mimi kept up her improvisational herding technique, slipping and sliding in the mud. Her tailbone hurt almost as much as her feet, though the cold wind and icy rain were effectively numbing both. Her teeth chattered and her nose ran. She bent every few steps to pick up another clod to keep the cow moving. She kept her gaze focused on the cow's tail, barely noticing when they finally reached the open gate.

"'Bout time you got here."

She looked up to see Garrett sitting comfortably astride his horse, seemingly oblivious to the wind and the rain and the cold.

She clenched her mouth shut to keep her lips from chattering, then pointed to the cow. "I got her."

"So I see." He turned to watch the cow amble peacefully along the worn grass trail they had followed to the pasture.

Mimi brushed her stringy, wet bangs out of her eyes. "Where's the rest of the herd?"

"I moved them already."

She blinked at him. "By yourself?"

He nodded. "They've been on the trail before. Once I get them out of the pasture, they pretty much know the way. They know there will be fresh hay waiting for them, too."

She'd just spent the past hour trying to get one cow out of the pasture, while Garrett had moved the entire rest of the herd all the way to the corral. She suddenly felt very tired.

He rode up beside her and extended his hand. "Need a lift?"

She grabbed his hand and let him pull her up behind him on the saddle. His horse shifted slightly at the extra weight, but settled quickly with a hushed word from Garrett.

Since she wasn't exactly in the mood to take another dive from a horse, she wrapped her arms firmly around Garrett's waist. His warmth quickly penetrated her slicker, and Mimi scooted even closer to him.

He turned his bay gelding and started following the cow.

"What about Pooh?" she asked, still slightly embarrassed that she'd lost her horse.

"We'll come back and get him after this last cow is safe in the corral. If a cow bolts once, they're likely to do it again, and I don't want to search all over the hill country for one stray cow."

"Aren't you afraid Pooh might run away?"

He shook his head, inadvertently causing the rain-water collecting in the brim of his cowboy hat to splash into her face. "Horses are loyal animals. He'll come home eventually."

She realized this wasn't the first time he'd spoken of loyalty and wondered why it was so important to him. But she was too tired and wet to ask. Nestling against his back, she laid her head on his shoulder and let her eyelids droop for a moment. It wasn't even noon yet, and she was completely exhausted.

The next thing she knew, Garrett was gently nudging her in the ribs with his elbow. "Hey, wake up. We're home."

She blinked and sat up straight, then let Garrett help her off the horse. *Home.* The word had never sounded so good. She hoped Garrett would build a huge, roaring fire.

"You go on in," he said. "I've got a few chores left to do."

She headed gratefully to the mud porch located at the back of the house. Not even bothering to hide her limp, she willed herself to take one step after another despite the pain in her feet. Once inside, she hung up her slicker, wiped her muddy boots on the mat. Then she looked into the small round mirror above the porch sink. The face looking back at her resembled something dragged out of a swamp.

One thing was for certain. Garrett Lord wouldn't be tempted to kiss her again.

GARRETT STOOD outside the mud porch, letting the rain wash down on him while he tried to get his body under control. He'd never been so aroused by a woman before. Especially not one who looked like a dirty, drowned kitten. But the way she'd pressed up against him in the saddle had sent his blood racing south. Her arms had been wrapped tightly around his waist, those slender, dainty hands only inches from the fly of his jeans.

He groaned under his breath and leaned against the back door of the house. When he'd made the deal with Mimi, he'd expected her to be the one to suffer. Not him. Granted, he knew he was attracted to her, but that kiss last night had ignited a fire inside him that refused to be quenched.

How the hell would he survive the next two days?

The answer was obvious. He wouldn't. Which meant he had to make her see what she was really in for as a ranch hand. He'd been going easy on her, expecting her to fold. She had gumption—he'd give her that.

He turned abruptly and stepped inside the mud porch, almost tripping over Mimi. She sat on an old rag rug, tugging hard on one of her muddy boots.

He folded his arms across his chest. "Having problems?"

"You could say that," she snapped, dropping her foot on the floor with a loud thud. "What took you so long?"

"I rode back to the pasture to get Pooh." He knelt beside her. "I take it you need some help."

She waved in frustration at her boots. "They're stuck."

"You should have told me they were too tight."

"They weren't until it started to rain," she retorted, as if the weather were his doing. Then she sighed. "All right, they were a little snug this morning when I put them on. My feet were swollen."

He frowned. "Why the hell didn't you tell me?"

"Because you'd think I was just making up an excuse to get out of working."

"You won't be any good to me at all if you're hobbled up." Guilt nibbled at him. He should have realized this might happen. Her feet had been torn up after walking barefoot to his ranch. And yesterday she'd broken in a new pair of boots. New to her, anyway.

"Just get them off," she whispered. Her muddy face was etched in misery, and her wet hair had come undone from its ponytail and hung in stringy tendrils around her cheeks.

He ran his fingers over the wet leather, then gripped the heel of one boot with both hands. She groaned low in her throat as he tugged hard, but the boot didn't move.

He rose to his feet. "We're going to have to do this the old-fashioned way."

She looked at him warily. "I don't think I like the sound of that."

He smiled. "It's not as bad as it sounds. In fact, you might enjoy it." While she sat on the floor, he straddled her outstretched legs, his back to her. "Okay, give me a foot."

She held up one foot between his legs and he grasped it with both hands. "Now what?"

"Now you need to apply some leverage. Put your other foot on my butt and push as hard as you can."

"You're right," she said as she followed his instructions, "I might enjoy this, after all."

He pulled while she pushed, and after several long seconds, the boot came off with a loud whoosh.

"We did it!" She held out her other booted foot and placed her stocking foot on his backside.

Garrett began pulling again, trying to ignore the way her slender foot molded to him. After what seemed an eternity, the second boot came off, as well.

Mimi slumped back on her bent elbows with a blissful sigh. "I think this is the happiest moment of my life."

"Sounds like you've had a pretty boring life." He held out a hand and hoisted her to her feet, noting how she winced as she walked into the kitchen.

"I've sure never appreciated the little things before," she said over her shoulder. "Like dry clothes and a warm house."

"Don't forget lunch."

She moved slowly toward the refrigerator. "I'll make us some sandwiches."

"You go change clothes," he ordered, moving toward the refrigerator. "I'll take care of lunch."

TWENTY MINUTES LATER she'd washed all the mud off her body and changed into a pair of clean denim jeans and a blue T-shirt. She left her sore feet bare, then padded to the laundry room to deposit her wet, mud-soaked clothes in the washing machine. By the time she returned to the kitchen, Garrett had set the table.

"Sit down," he ordered, placing a loaf of fragrant garlic bread on the table.

"This isn't fair," she said, reluctantly taking a seat in the nearest kitchen chair. "I'm willing to do my part. I'll bet you don't normally serve your ranch hands lunch."

"Actually, we take turns. When I hire on a cowboy, all I expect him to do is to help take care of the ranch, not take care of me. Sharing the cooking duties just saves us both time in the long run."

"So you'll let me make lunch tomorrow?"

"Definitely." He sat opposite her. "As long as you don't make meat loaf. I've never been partial to meat loaf."

"You've got it, cowboy." She rested her chin on her hands. "So what are we having today?"

He took a sip of his iced tea. "Lasagna."

She blinked. "Lasagna? When exactly did you find the time to make lasagna?"

"I do a lot of cooking and freezing before calving season. It's a busy time, so it's either prepare ahead or get used to a lot of peanut butter sandwiches."

"I'm very impressed."

"Wait until you taste it," he said, setting down his glass. "You might change your mind."

"At the moment, I could eat a horse." She grinned. "No, make that a cow. Specifically, the one who wanted to play tag with me today."

"The important thing is that you won," he said, then laughed. "That poor cow never had a chance once you started flinging those cow patties. You've got a good arm."

"Cow patties?" she said weakly. "You mean…"

His grin widened. "Are you telling me you didn't know what they were?"

"I thought they were dirt clods." She licked her lips, feeling a hot blush crawl up her cheeks. "I mean, I know they were a little flat, but I figured that was from the cows stepping on them."

"Welcome to life on the range, Mimi. We call them cow pies." Then he held up both hands. "But please don't cook those for lunch tomorrow, either."

"Very funny," she muttered, feeling like a complete fool. "I can't believe I touched cow…"

"Turds. Manure. Shi—"

"I get it." She bit the words out, her cheeks aflame.

"You should see your face." His deep laughter filled the room.

She liked the sound of it, even though she wasn't thrilled at the reason for it. "It's not that funny."

"Don't worry, Mimi. It may be the first time you touch cow manure, but it sure won't be the last." He arched a brow. "Unless you've had enough?"

She was almost tempted to tell him yes. But he looked too damn confident. Even though she'd just experienced the most miserable morning of her life, she wasn't ready to give up yet. "I'm here to stay, Garrett. At least, for the next few weeks."

He leaned back in his chair and folded his arms across his broad chest. His face was ruggedly handsome, from his chiseled square jaw to the small scar above his left eyebrow. Mimi realized she could look at him all day. He was an endangered species—a real cowboy.

"You don't believe me?" she asked at last.

He shrugged. "You've got two days left, Mimi. And it's not going to get any easier."

She tipped up her chin. "I can handle it."

He rose and walked to the stove, picking up a hot pad before opening the oven door and pulling out the steaming casserole dish.

Her mouth watered at the fragrant aroma. Lunch at

the Casville house usually meant watercress sandwiches or simple fruit salad. Something light and not
too filling. She looked at the savory lasagna steaming
in the eight-inch-square casserole dish and hoped it
would be enough for both of them.

He'd barely set it on the trivet when she picked up
the serving spoon and helped herself to a man-size
portion.

Garrett moved to the sink and began filling an old
tin kettle with water.

Mimi picked up her fork and held it poised over
her plate. But the impeccable table manners her
mother had taught her forbade her from taking that
first bite until Garrett was seated at the table. "Aren't
you going to eat?"

"In a minute," he said, carrying the kettle over to
her. He set it on the floor by her chair. "Put your feet
in here and let them soak while you eat."

"You like to give orders, don't you?" she said,
touched and more than a little surprised that a man
like Garrett could be so thoughtful. She did as he in-
structed, swallowing a moan of pleasure as the
warmth of the water penetrated her sore, tired feet.

"I should order you in bed for the rest of the day,"
he grumbled, sitting down and helping himself to lasagna.

"No way," she countered, forking up her first bite
of the gooey pasta. "I'm fine."

"Like hell." He reached for a slice of garlic bread.
"I never should have agreed to this deal. You aren't
cut out for this kind of work."

Mimi's heart skipped a beat. What if he backed out
of their deal? What if he insisted on taking her to

Austin this afternoon? She needed to change the subject. Fast.

She looked at him. ''Tell me about the teddy bear in your room.''

CHAPTER FIVE

"THE TEDDY BEAR?" A muscle ticked in Garrett's jaw. "What about it?"

Mimi instinctively knew she'd hit a nerve. Which made her even more curious. "It looks very old. How long have you had it?"

"About four months."

"Then you must be a collector. I'm not an expert, but that bear is quite unusual."

"You can say that again," he muttered, then turned his attention to his lunch. She watched him fork up his lasagna in big chunks. Neither one of them said anything for several long minutes, the only sound that of forks scraping against plates.

At last, he looked at her. "It's no big deal. That teddy bear supposedly belonged to me when I was a baby."

"Supposedly?"

He set down his fork. "If you want to know the whole sordid story, my mother abandoned us when I was two and a half years old and my brother and sisters were just babies. She left us on the steps of the Maitland Maternity Clinic and took off."

Mimi had heard of the renowned clinic. It had been founded in Austin over two and a half decades ago, and its sterling reputation brought in clients from all over the country, including many celebrities.

Garrett crumpled his paper napkin and tossed it on his plate. "She threw us away like yesterday's garbage, with nothing more than our first names pinned to our clothes."

Mimi flinched at his harsh words. They pricked her more than she wanted to admit. For reasons she didn't want to remember. "Did you ever see your birth mother again?"

He shook his head. "No. And that was twenty-five years ago. If it wasn't for Megan Maitland, I don't know what would have happened to us."

Mimi had heard a lot about Megan Maitland, but she'd never met the matriarch of the Maitland clan. "Is she the one who found you?"

He nodded. "She took us in, then contacted the Lords. They desperately wanted children but couldn't have any of their own."

"So your mother's sacrifice was their blessing," Mimi said softly.

"Sacrifice?" Garrett snorted. "Try selfishness. She abandoned us on that step and never looked back. We hadn't heard one word from her until a few months ago. That's when she sent that damn bear to Aunt Megan, along with three tiny baby sweaters that had belonged to Michael, Shelby and Lana."

So that explained the raw emotion in his voice. His birth mother had reopened an old wound. For a man of few words, his hurt had poured out of him. She'd never heard him talk so much as he had in the last few moments. But then, Garrett didn't strike her as a man who kept secrets.

Mimi had kept a secret of her own locked in her heart for over ten years. A secret she'd never told anyone, not even her father. Sometimes secrets were for the best.

But a man like Garrett wouldn't understand that. He had simple values. Hard work. Loyalty. Honesty.

Her conscience pricked when she remembered how she'd lied to him about her name. She hadn't told him about her family or her background, either, although that was more a lie of omission. His deep voice penetrated her musings, and to her chagrin, she realized she'd missed some of his story.

"So we decided to look for her," he said, pushing his plate away. "Only it seems we've hit a dead end."

"Your mother didn't leave any clues when she sent the teddy bear and the sweaters? No address or phone number?"

"Nope."

"Have you thought about hiring a private detective?"

He nodded. "We had one for a while. But he was better at racking up his bill than finding our mother. Although through a process of elimination we were able to discover her name, LeeAnn Larrimore."

She hesitated, hoping he wouldn't find her suggestion intrusive. "Maybe I could help."

One corner of his mouth quirked in a smile. "Are you a better detective than you are a cowgirl?"

"No, but I'm a damn good archivist."

For the first time since she'd met him, Garrett looked perplexed. "What exactly is an archivist?"

She smiled, quite used to that question. Her father had asked it when she'd announced her career intentions. Paul had found her job choice amusing. "An archivist collects and organizes historical records and artifacts."

"So you work in a museum."

"I used to, but right now I'm working in the private sector. I'm putting together an extensive genealogy and historical archives for...a prominent Austin family." Another lie by omission. But for some reason she couldn't bring herself to tell him that family was her own—the rich and powerful Casvilles.

"Sounds impressive. But how could you help me?"

Mimi leaned forward. "You've been searching for your mother in the present, during her lifetime. I'll look for her by searching the past. If we can find her family roots, we have a good chance of locating her. I'll start by checking out birth records, marriage licenses and obituaries for matches to the name Larrimore. Then there are historical societies, genealogy clubs, old newspapers. The possibilities are almost endless."

"So part of your job is tracking down missing persons?"

"Well, not exactly. I've never done anything like this before. I sure couldn't make you any promises."

He picked up his glass of iced tea and drained it. Then he stood up. "Thanks for the offer, Mimi, but it sounds like a lot of work to me. And you'll only be here for another day or two."

She opened her mouth to argue with him, but he didn't give her a chance.

"I need to run into Austin and buy some parts for the tractor." He walked toward the back door. "I'm expecting a call from a man who's interested in buying one of the bulls. So I'd like you to stay inside this afternoon in case he phones. Tell him I've got five premium Texas longhorn bulls ready for service. I'll call him back tonight if he's interested."

"All right." Mimi's feet hurt too much to argue, even though she suspected the important phone call was just an excuse to make her rest. Despite his gruff exterior, she was slowly discovering, Garrett Lord had a tender heart.

"I'll see you around six," he said, grabbing his cowboy hat off the peg by the door. "And I'll bring supper home with me. I can't go into town without bringing back a big bucket of crispy fried chicken."

She smiled as he walked out the door, then her smile faded. Despite his matter-of-fact attitude, she'd seen the hurt in his eyes when he'd talked about his mother. And she *could* help him find her. In fact, she suspected Garrett had the key that would unlock the door to his past right here in this house.

That key was his old teddy bear.

PAUL RENQUIST checked his watch for the third time in ten minutes. Harper was late. Rain drummed against the windowpanes of one of the trendiest restaurants in Austin. He matched the beat with his manicured fingers against the tabletop, growing more irritated with each passing minute. Nobody was ever late for a meeting with Rupert Casville. Yet people always kept Paul waiting.

No one gave him the respect he deserved.

Like Mimi. The more he thought about her defection, the angrier he got. How dare she leave him stranded at the altar. How dare she make him look like an idiot in front of Austin's elite. A bunch of stuffed shirts who were probably laughing at him behind his back.

Damn, he needed a drink.

He rubbed one hand over the back of his neck, wishing he knew what Mimi was thinking right now. What if she showed up, but refused to marry him? He'd been confident in his ability to woo her into rational thinking, but the longer she stayed away, the more his confidence ebbed.

Harper finally appeared, hailing him from across the room while he handed his wet leather bomber jacket to the coat-check woman.

Paul ground his teeth, wishing like hell he could order a whiskey from the bar. He liked them straight up. His tongue tingled just thinking about it.

"Sorry I'm late," Harper said as he approached the table. He sat down, raking his damp blond hair with one hand. "Traffic is backed up because of that damn construction on Lamar Boulevard."

Paul didn't like excuses. "Don't let it happen again."

Amusement flashed in Harper's green eyes as he gave a mock salute. "Yes, sir."

A waitress appeared at the table, giving Paul her best smile. She was pretty, in a generic sort of way. But he didn't have time to waste with her. Besides, once he had his hands on some of that Casville money, he could have any woman he wanted.

"I'll have a bourbon and water," Harper ordered.

"And you, sir?" she asked, turning to Paul with a seductive swing of her hips.

But the only seduction that enticed him at the moment came out of a liquor bottle. Why the hell had he picked a restaurant that served alcohol? He took a deep breath.

"Nothing for me."

Her smile dimmed a few watts, then she nodded and walked away.

"Well?" Paul asked, tired of playing the waiting game. "What's the latest on Mimi?"

Harper shook his head. "That lady knows how to disappear. There's no sign of her. I mean nothing. She hasn't touched her credit cards or her bank account. None of her friends have heard a word from her. It's like she disappeared into thin air."

"She's got to be somewhere," Paul countered. "Did you check the car lots? Maybe she traded in her convertible for something more anonymous."

Harper shrugged. "I suppose it's possible. We could make her disappearance public and ask for anyone with information to come forward. If we offered a reward, we'd probably have eyewitnesses popping out of the woodwork."

"No," Paul said quickly. A little too quickly. He took a deep breath. "Her father thinks we should keep this quiet. You know how the media will eat up this story if they get a sniff of it."

Harper nodded. "Then I say we just sit back and wait. My guess is that she'll show up eventually. A rich, spoiled princess won't last long in the real world. As soon as she needs a manicure, she'll come running back home."

"I'm not willing to wait that long." He lowered his voice. "I want her found, Harper. And I don't care if you have to break a few laws to do it."

The waitress arrived with Harper's drink. "Will there be anything else?"

"No," Paul said shortly, holding out his hand for the bill.

She gave it to him, then walked away.

"One more thing," Paul said, his gaze drifting to the beautiful amber-colored whiskey. "I want you to delve into Mimi's background. See if you can dig up any dirt."

"No problem." Harper sat back in his chair, his expression thoughtful. "I do have some methods I haven't employed yet. But they're expensive, Paul. Very expensive."

"To hell with the cost," Paul said, struggling to maintain his composure. He took a deep, calming breath. "I'm not sure you understand the seriousness of this situation. Rupert Casville is not a well man. And the stress caused by his daughter's disappearance hasn't helped him any."

Harper nodded, his mouth curved in a wry smile. "So this is a medical emergency?"

Paul leaned back in his chair, calmer. "You could say that. He's put me in charge, by the way, so if you come up with any information, or better yet, actually find her, you come to me. Leave Rupert completely out of the loop. Got it?"

"Loud and clear." Harper picked up his drink. "Of course, you get what you pay for. The more *incentive* you give me to find her, the quicker I can get the job done."

Hell. Paul reached inside his suit coat for his checkbook. The temptation to fire Harper for his insolence was almost overwhelming. But what choice did he have? He might need a man short on ethics to see this job through to the end.

"How much do you need?"

MIMI HUNG UP the telephone, excitement zinging through her veins. After two hours, she'd finally reached Dr. Hawkins, an associate professor at Texas A&M University. He taught Texas history, and collecting local antique toys was one of his hobbies. On weekends, he traveled to antique road shows to give his expert opinion on family heirlooms. He shared his experiences with his classes, telling them many people had a small fortune in their attic and didn't even know it.

She knew as soon as she'd seen Garrett's teddy bear that it was unusual. She hadn't realized how unusual until she'd described it in detail to Dr. Hawkins.

He'd told her to give him three days before she called him again. By then, he should have the information she wanted. Three days. That seemed to be the magic number lately. Unfortunately, she only had one day left to prove herself to Garrett. What if she thought she could do the job, but he didn't agree? They hadn't stipulated exactly how she could win the job.

She looked around the cozy living room as rain pattered on the roof. It was starkly neat, but she could see a fine layer of dust on the end tables and the fireplace mantel. If Garrett expected a ranch hand to pitch in with the cooking, maybe he expected one to pitch in with the dusting, as well.

It wasn't until Mimi was kneeling in front of the cupboard under the kitchen sink that she realized how complicated this dusting business could be. Growing up in her father's house, she'd taken the more mundane upkeep of a home for granted. The maids kept the Casville mansion spotless almost as if by magic.

Or was it by lemon Pledge? She picked up the can and read the label. Then she picked up the bottle of Murphy's Oil Soap and compared the two. At last she decided to wash everything down with the soap first, then follow with the furniture polish. She grabbed an empty bucket out of the cupboard, filled it with warm water, then added two capfuls of the soap.

With washcloth in hand, she carried it to the living room and got to work. An hour later, she looked around with pride. Every surface glistened. Except one.

She frowned at the old stone fireplace. The sooty hearth looked as if it hadn't been cleaned since the house was built. Which, according to Garrett, had been sometime in the early fifties.

After refilling her bucket with warm, soapy water, she tackled the job. It was much harder than it looked. The soot had formed layers on the old stone hearth, and it took more than a little elbow grease to scrub it off. It also blackened everything it touched, including her hands and arms. When her nose started to itch, she scratched without thinking, then made matters worse by brushing the hair off her forehead.

"Cinderella, I presume?"

Mimi started at the sound of the amused feminine voice, then turned to see Venna Schwab framed in the doorway. Her thick, dark brown hair was neatly parted into two long braids. But her bright red lips and the too-tight blue jeans and low-cut red peasant blouse belied the girlish image she was trying to portray.

Venna shut the door behind her, then took off her cowboy hat, shaking the water off the brim before hanging it on the peg by the door. "I knocked, but you must not have heard me. That rain is really coming down."

Mimi dropped the washrag in the bucket and hastily stood, wiping her dirty hands on the front of her jeans. "Garrett's not here."

"I know," Venna said, walking toward her. "His pickup truck isn't in the driveway. But I know he won't want to miss my fresh baked apple pie." She held up the round plastic container in her hands.

Mimi took a step forward. "I can take it for you."

Venna wrinkled her nose at the sight of Mimi's soot-stained fingers. "That's all right. I know my way around here."

She sailed into the kitchen with the pie while Mimi followed, trying to finger comb her hair into obedience. Venna looked perfect, despite the rainstorm. But her ostrich-skin cowboy boots were trailing rainwater and mud all over Mimi's clean floor.

"Can I get you something?" Mimi asked politely. "A cup of coffee or a glass of iced tea?"

"No, thank you. I really can't stay." Venna set the container on the counter and opened the lid. The spicy scent of cinnamon and apples filled the air.

"That smells delicious."

Venna smiled as she pulled the pie out of the container. "Apple pie is Garrett's favorite."

For some reason, the way Venna said Garrett's name rankled Mimi. It was so...proprietary.

"So," Venna said, turning and leaning her back against the counter. She swept Mimi up and down with a quick, dismissive glance. "I take it you've given up ranch work to become Garrett's house-keeper."

"No, I'm still his ranch hand," Mimi said, walking to the sink to wash the sticky soot off her hands. She pumped a generous dollop of soap into her hands from the dispenser, then turned on the tap water. "In fact, we moved the herd out of the north pasture this morn-ing."

"You don't look much like a ranch hand," Venna said amiably.

"I guess appearances can be deceiving." Mimi turned off the tap, then reached for a towel.

Venna arched a finely winged brow. "Did he tell you about me?"

"He said you were a neighbor."

She laughed. "He's not a man of many words, is he? We're much closer than neighbors."

"Really?" Mimi knew she shouldn't pry. The man's personal life was none of her business. But she couldn't seem to help herself. "How close?"

"Garrett asked me to marry him."

Mimi had her answer. An answer she didn't want to hear.

IT WAS almost dusk by the time Garrett arrived at the ranch. His trip into Austin had been an unqualified disaster. First, he'd arrived at the John Deere dealer-ship to discover that the tractor part he'd ordered had been mistakenly shipped to Nebraska. Then he'd stopped by his sister Shelby's diner, Austin Eats, for a quick bite.

Shelby was just as frustrated as Garrett that the search for their birth mother had stalled. She'd even wondered aloud if it was time to give up. But Garrett couldn't quit. Couldn't just forget the woman who had given birth to him, then given him up. He had to know why. He had to know what had driven her to leave her children on a stranger's doorstep.

All his life, he'd felt incomplete. Like something was missing. Something important. But he hadn't connected his emptiness with his birth mother until that teddy bear and those baby sweaters had shown up. He still sometimes wondered if Aunt Megan was telling them everything she knew. He respected her more than any other woman, but he also believed she'd keep a secret if she thought it would protect the people she cared about.

He walked through the front door of the house, wiping his boots on the braided rug. A strange, lemony scent invaded his nostrils. He smelled cinnamon, too, along with the strong odor of soap.

"Mimi?"

No answer. He walked halfway down the hall, then heard the sound of the shower running. Along with an off-key version of "You Are My Sunshine." He smiled as he headed to the living room. She must be tired of the rain, too.

A cheerful fire burned in the hearth, melting that cold, empty place inside him. For one brief moment, he savored the feeling of coming home to a warm house and a woman singing in his shower.

He imagined her all soft and wet and soapy. Her

sky-blue eyes sparkling and her hair slicked off her freshly washed face. Mimi hadn't worn any makeup since the day she'd shown up in his hayloft. Probably because she didn't have any. He preferred her natural color, anyway. Her soft, creamy complexion. Her rosy cheeks. Even her red, peeling, sunburned nose.

The water stopped running, and Garrett headed into the kitchen to put more distance between himself and his current fantasy. The worst thing he could do was act on these insane desires. Not when Mimi would most likely be gone tomorrow. He'd had his share of one-night stands when he was younger, and the idea didn't appeal to him anymore. It seemed to magnify the emptiness inside of him.

His good intentions were rewarded when he found the apple pie sitting on the counter. The flaky, golden-brown crust was etched with little hearts. Worry niggled at him.

Were the hearts a message? Had Mimi been having some fantasies of her own? His heart skipped a beat at the thought. Part of him liked the idea. Another part of him worried that her fiancé would show up with a shotgun and demand his woman back. Garrett had already been shot once this year because of a woman. That was more than enough for him.

"You're back."

He turned to see Mimi framed in the kitchen door. She'd wrapped herself in his blue terry-cloth robe, and her face was flushed from her shower. Her blond hair hung in ringlets around her head, and her blue eyes looked all soft and dewy.

His body's instant response to her appearance took him off guard. He turned to the pie on the counter, pulling out a knife from the drawer to cut himself a thick slab. "I see you've made yourself at home."

"I borrowed your robe," she said, moving closer to him. "I hope you don't mind."

"No problem," he said, envying a robe for the first time in his life.

She wrapped her hands around the collar and pulled it tighter. "It's chilly in here."

"You'll be warmer when you get dressed." He carried his pie to the kitchen table and sat down, making a concerted effort not to look at her.

"Is something wrong?" she asked softly.

"It's been a hell of a day," he muttered, digging into his pie. No doubt his night was ruined, as well. He wouldn't get any sleep with images of her in his head.

She padded to the table and took a seat opposite him. "I had a visitor while you were gone."

He let the sweet and spicy flavors of the apple pie linger on his tongue. "Who?"

"Your…neighbor. Venna. She's the one who made the pie."

His fork froze in midair. Well, that explained the hearts. It also made him realize that his day could have been worse. He could have arrived home and found Venna Schwab encamped in his kitchen.

Mimi licked her lips. "Is there something you want to tell me?"

His brows drew together at the question. "No. I don't think so."

She took a deep breath. "Something about Venna?"

He forked up another bite of pie. "No."

Mimi fingered the collar of his robe, plucking at the tiny terry-cloth strands. His gaze lingered for a moment, mesmerized by the delicate, creamy skin outlined by the vee of the robe. She looked so soft. So warm.

"Garrett?"

He blinked and looked at her. A rare flush prickled his cheeks at the turn his thoughts had taken. *Damn.* He had to get out of here. He was losing control, and Garrett Lord never lost control. "What?"

Mimi leaned forward. A big mistake. The robe gapped slightly at the movement, and he could see the generous curve of one breast. His breath caught and his body grew unbearably tight.

"Venna told me you asked her to marry you."

He barely registered her words, too entranced by the drop of water trickling down her neck, past her collarbone, into the vee of her breasts. Pushing his chair back, he hastily rose to his feet. "I need to go check the horses. Help yourself to the chicken."

"But..."

He was out the door before she got another word out of her mouth. Rain pelted him, soaking through his clothes, but he didn't dare go back for his slicker. Not when he was so close to the edge of losing control. Not when he wanted to pull her against him and see if the sizzle of that first kiss could erupt into an inferno.

He ran the last few steps to the barn, diving through the door and spooking the horses and the barn swallows already settled in for the night. Raindrops battered against the tin roof, making it sound as if stones fell from the sky instead of the sorely needed moisture.

He brushed the water off his clothes, then moved quietly to Brutus's stall to give him his nightly ration of oats. While the gelding stood contentedly chewing, Garrett picked up the currycomb hanging on a hook and began brushing him.

Brutus gave a whinny of delight. The easy rhythm of the familiar chore slowed Garrett's heartbeat and eased his taut nerves. This situation was getting out of hand. When he'd agreed to Mimi's deal, he'd expected her to turn tail and run back to Austin before the sun had set. But she had surprised him. She'd also turned out to be much more determined and stubborn than he'd ever imagined.

One thing was certain. He couldn't go on like this. Wanting her every minute of every day was driving him to distraction. And he couldn't have her, he reminded himself. Not when she belonged to another man.

The only way to end this torture was to win their wager so he could send her back to Austin.

It was time to take more drastic measures.

CHAPTER SIX

THE NEXT MORNING, Mimi pulled the pillow over her head when she heard the dreaded knock on the bedroom door. The warmth of the bed quickly lured her back to sleep. Then the knock sounded again, only louder.

She groaned into the mattress, then raised her head up far enough to squint at the glowing red numbers on the digital clock beside the bed. Two o'clock. She blinked and looked again. She knew Garrett didn't believe in wasting daylight, but this was ridiculous.

"Let's go, Mimi," he shouted, pounding on the door once more. "You don't want me to have to come in there to get you."

Something about his tone more than the words themselves made her stumble out of bed and reach for her clothes. "I'm up," she called, stepping clumsily into her blue jeans.

"Meet me at the corral," he ordered through the door.

Her heavy eyelids drifted shut as her fingers fumbled with the buttons on her shirt. Didn't the man ever sleep? Mimi had stayed up past eleven o'clock waiting for him to come in from the barn. But the long day had finally caught up with her, and she'd dragged herself off to bed, her mind still full of unanswered questions.

It was obvious the subject of Venna was off-limits. She'd been surprised at his odd reaction. Garrett was one of the most honest and forthright men she'd ever met, yet he'd practically run out the door just to avoid talking to her.

Sore subject, perhaps. Or, more likely, none of her business. She was his ranch hand, not his confidante. What Garrett did after hours was none of her concern.

But the thought of him spending those hours with Venna pricked at her like a sandbur. She couldn't blame him for finding the woman attractive. And he obviously liked her cooking. No doubt Venna Schwab would make the perfect ranch wife.

So why did the idea bother Mimi so much?

The rain had stopped, so she grabbed a pair of insulated coveralls instead of a slicker. She stepped into them, then zipped them up the front. What they lacked in style they made up for in warmth and durability. She took a moment to cuff the long pant legs around her ankles, then stepped outside. A coyote serenade met her, sending a tiny shiver up her spine.

The ranch seemed so different at night, almost foreign. Glancing over her shoulder at the house, she thought longingly of her warm bed. Then she turned, squared her shoulders and strode toward the corral.

"I didn't want you to miss all the fun," Garrett said as she walked up to the split-rail fence.

"What fun?"

He nodded toward the south end of the corral. "The first calf of the season."

Mimi's breath caught in her throat at the sight of

the lone cow standing there with the thin trail of mucous hanging from her back end. Her belly was so distended, Mimi wondered how the cow could stand upright. "You mean she's going to have her calf here? Now?"

"It might take a little while," he replied. "But it's definitely going to happen tonight."

She stared in wonder at the straining cow. Excitement and anticipation erased the last remnants of sleepiness from her body.

Garrett glanced at her. "Good thing you wore those old coveralls."

"Why?"

"There's going to be a lot of blood."

Her anticipation turned to apprehension, and her mouth suddenly went very dry. She swallowed hard. "Blood?"

"Birthing is a very messy business," he said matter-of-factly.

She closed her eyes, wondering how she could have been so dense. Garrett had hired her for calving season. It should have been obvious that she'd have to witness some births before she was through.

And as she knew very well, births meant blood.

Why hadn't she realized this might be a problem when she made that stupid deal? She might be naive, but she wasn't dumb.

"Anything wrong?"

She looked into his face, illuminated by the overhead mercury lamp. "No, of course not. What could be wrong?"

He shrugged and turned to the corral. "I don't know. You look a little pale."

Her hands gripped the rough wooden rail. She'd probably faint at the first sign of blood. Then he'd have the perfect excuse to ship her back to Austin as soon as the sun came up.

She wasn't ready to go.

When Garrett turned toward the calf, she studied him in the moonlight. For some reason, she couldn't put that kiss they'd shared the other night out of her mind. More than once she'd wondered what would have happened if Garrett hadn't stopped. What did she want to happen?

Mimi knew what she didn't want. She didn't want to go back to Austin yet. The thought of facing her father and Paul made her feel ill. She knew it was cowardly to hide out from them like this, but she just needed more time. Time to heal. Time to figure out what to do with the rest of her life.

"Looks like it will be any time now," Garrett mused, still watching the cow. "I brought the calf pullers in case she has any trouble."

Mimi didn't like the sound of that. "Calf pullers?"

He pointed to an odd metal contraption in the back of his pickup truck. "Sometimes the calf is too big for the cow to push through the birth canal. That's when we hook the chain onto one of the calf's legs and turn the crank."

She winced in sympathy for the cow. Just the thought of such a procedure made her feel woozy. How could she ever witness it, much less participate in it?

"I need to sit down."

He hitched one boot up on the fence. "Plenty of ground here to do it on."

Her knees gave out, and she plopped onto the grass, taking deep, gulping breaths. Fortunately, Garrett seemed oblivious to her distress. But if she passed out or threw up, he'd soon be aware of it.

"Of course, the calf pullers don't always work," Garrett continued. "Then I have to call the vet out to do an emergency C-section. If we're lucky, both the cow and the calf survive. But it does leave the cow with a big scar on her belly."

Mimi's hand drifted toward her stomach. She knew all about scars.

"I remember one time," Garrett said, gazing into the corral, "we had six cows calving at the same time, and they were all in distress. I spent the entire night running from cow to cow with my calf pullers. It was a real mess."

Her head spun. She closed her eyes and tried to regain her equilibrium. *I can do this,* she mouthed to herself over and over again like a mantra.

"I doubt that will happen tonight," he said, seemingly oblivious to her state. "But you never know. That's one calving season I'll never forget."

She tried not to listen, but the man wouldn't stop talking. For a brief moment, she wondered if he'd been drinking. She hadn't realized Garrett Lord had this many words in him. Unfortunately, he told her much more than she wanted to know about calving complications, retained placentas and udder infections.

Her stomach twisted and her head reeled and she hadn't even seen any blood yet. She wondered if she should just admit defeat now while she still had a little pride left. Even if it meant going back to Austin. Even if it meant never seeing Garrett Lord again.

"Mimi?" he whispered.

He stood with his hand out to her. She reached up and grabbed it almost without thinking and let him pull her to her feet.

He nudged her in front of him, his breath warm on her cheek. "It's time."

She moved closer to the fence, her knees rubbery and her eyes unfocused. Despite her trepidation, she couldn't help but look at the cow. Among the mucus and the blood was something she'd completely forgotten. Something that made her stare in wonder and amazement. Something that made her breath catch in her throat.

A baby calf struggling to find its way into the world.

The head had emerged, slick and wet. After several strained pushes from the cow, the bony shoulders followed. Then, amazingly, the rest of the calf slipped free. It lay on the ground, the tiny, wet body quivering.

Mimi looked at Garrett, her throat too tight with emotion to speak. At some time during the ordeal, she'd clutched his arm. She stared at her fingers, wrapped around his biceps. She could feel the bulge of his muscle and the warmth of his skin through his sleeve.

She looked into his eyes, her voice as shaky as her body. "Isn't that the most beautiful thing you've ever seen?"

"Almost," he said huskily, his gaze not on the calf anymore, but on her.

Her knees went weak again. This time for an entirely different reason. For the space of one heartbeat she wondered if he was going to kiss her again. In the next heartbeat, she realized she wanted him to kiss her.

But instead of moving closer to her, Garrett backed away, then turned his attention to the corral once again. "Looks like we're done here for tonight."

Mimi reluctantly turned from him and saw the cow licking her new calf with long, gentle strokes of her tongue. "It's amazing, isn't it?"

Garrett didn't say anything for a long moment. "No matter how many times I witness it, birth is always a miracle."

She nodded, hot tears stinging her eyes.

The calf wobbled as it tried to rise on its spindly legs. It didn't make it the first time. Or the second. The calf hit the ground numerous times before it finally succeeded in standing. Despite its efforts, the mama cow kept up her ministrations, licking her calf clean.

Mimi smiled. "You can tell she loves it already."

"Sometimes they don't," Garrett said, his voice sounding a littler gruffer. A little more like normal. "Some cows reject their calves the moment they're born. They won't clean them or let them milk. They'd just leave them to die if I didn't intervene."

"But why?"

He shrugged his broad shoulders. "No maternal instinct, I guess. Not all females have one. Including the human kind."

Mimi recoiled as if she'd been slapped. But Garrett had already turned and begun walking toward his truck. There was enough light for her to see the pain etched on his face. *He'd been referring to his birth mother.* After all these years, it was obvious her abandonment still bothered him. Maybe that was why he was so desperate to find her.

Maybe Mimi could help him.

"You can go on back to the house," he said, opening the driver's door of the truck. He didn't look upset anymore, just very tired.

"What are you going to do?"

He nodded toward the calf pullers and the other paraphernalia in the back of the pickup. "I'll just unload this stuff in the tack room, then I'll be in, too."

"Let me do it," she said, moving toward him. "That's the reason I'm here, after all."

He hesitated, then shrugged and opened the driver's door of the pickup for her."

She climbed behind the steering wheel. "Where do you want me to put all this stuff?"

"Normally, I wash and sterilize the equipment, but since we didn't use anything, that won't be necessary tonight. Just hang it up on the hooks in the tack room."

"Anything else I should do?" Mimi asked as she switched on the ignition.

"Get a good night's sleep," Garrett replied. "We've got a long day ahead of us tomorrow." He closed the driver's door, then turned toward the house.

She watched him for a long moment, then shifted the truck into gear. Hubert, who had disappeared during the calving to chase jackrabbits, reappeared and escorted her to the barn, trotting beside the pickup.

"Quiet down," Mimi whispered to him after she

cut the engine and climbed out of the pickup. "You'll spook the horses."

Hubert followed cheerfully as she walked to the back of the truck and opened the tailgate. "You're awfully chipper for three o'clock in the morning," she said, unloading the calf pullers, a spray bottle of iodine and a bag full of vet supplies.

Hubert barked once, then waited while she pulled open the barn door. A horse whinnied inside, alerting the rest of the barn's occupants to her presence. Moist warmth and the strong scent of hay enveloped her as she carried the calving equipment inside the barn. Hubert chose to stay by the open barn door, walking back and forth to guard against intruders.

Mimi opened the door to the tack room, then switched on the light. She blinked at the brightness of the bare bulb hanging on a wire from the ceiling, then carried the calf pullers to the new pine shelves on the south wall.

Garrett had been expanding the tack room, making it big enough to hold the small refrigerator he needed for penicillin and other veterinary medications. The north wall was only half-done. He'd torn down the plywood walls, revealing the original studs and the old lath slats.

Mimi reached up to hang the bag of supplies on a bent nail above her, but the frayed strap slipped off her fingers and the bag fell to the floor. Syringes rolled onto the plank floor, along with a spool of black suture thread. Muttering an oath under her breath, she kneeled to gather everything into the bag.

She'd just reached for the last syringe when she saw something unusual. A dusty, worn red leather

book, tucked between a floorboard and one of the
studs on the north wall. After placing the bag on the
hook, she daintily pulled the book from its hiding
place, grimacing at the cobwebs clinging to it. She
blew the dust off the cover, then gently opened it. The
pages were aged and brittle, the gilt edges worn almost bare. But the gently flowing script was still leg-
ible.

The inside front cover read, *Private Property of
Miss Katherine MacGuire,* with the word *private* un-
derlined three times. Fascinated by the discovery of
this unexpected treasure, Mimi sank to the floor and
began reading.

> October 23, 1898
> I woke up this morning to the most beautiful
> lightning storm. Pa says it's God's way of wish-
> ing me happy birthday. I'm eighteen now, and
> Mama gave me this journal to record the joys
> and sorrows of my life. I pray the Lord sees fit
> to send some joy my way soon and save the sor-
> row for when I'm an old woman.

Mimi smiled as she turned the page. She wondered
if Katherine had penned her journal in this very barn
over one hundred years ago.

> November 1, 1898
> Pa hired on a new cowboy today. His name is
> Boyd Harrison and he's got the bluest eyes in
> Texas. He didn't give me a second glance, but I
> looked him over plenty while he was helping

break in the new lot of mustangs.

He hails from Kansas, but says he likes Texas better. Mama says he's the wandering kind. I hope he decides to stay here awhile.

"Watch out for those cowboys," Mimi warned softly under her breath. Then she turned to the next journal entry.

November 26, 1898

Mama invited all the hands to Thanksgiving dinner. I baked a chocolate cake and helped Mama cook up a mess of prairie chickens and dumplings. We also served candied sweet potatoes, succotash, and opened up two cans of watermelon pickles. Boyd said chocolate cake is his favorite.

It was the best Thanksgiving I can remember.

December 5, 1898

Boyd Harrison kissed me today behind the hog shed. His mustache tickled a little and he stopped kissing me when I started to laugh. He thought I was making fun of him until I told him the truth. Then he kissed me again. I liked it even better the second time.

Mimi heard a high-pitched whine and finally looked up from the old journal. Hubert sat at her feet, wagging his cropped tail.

"Did you get tired of waiting for me?" she asked, rising to her feet. She looked around the tack room, orienting herself once again to the present. Then she gently placed the journal in the oversize pocket of the coveralls. Giddy excitement washed through her at the discovery. As an archivist, she found this old journal more valuable than a pot of gold.

Whistling for Hubert to follow, she turned off the light in the tack room, then walked out the barn door, pulling it shut behind her. The mercury light illuminated the path to the house, and Mimi could feel the weight of the journal in her pocket as she walked.

It was strange to think that the author was a girl of eighteen who had at one time lived on this very ranch. She must have hidden her journal in the barn. No doubt to keep it out of reach of nosy brothers and sisters. Or perhaps her mother, who didn't sound as enthusiastic about the dashing Boyd Harrison as Katherine.

Reading about the young girl's troubles made her think of her own problems. Her family. Her father might be autocratic and high-handed. Might have lied to her. But she knew deep down that despite all his faults, he did love her. And she loved him, even if she wasn't ready to confront him yet.

As Mimi walked into the silent house and hung up her coveralls on the hook by the door, she wondered if her father was worried about her. And even more important, if he was taking good care of himself.

She carefully pulled the old journal from the pocket of the coveralls, then walked to the bedroom. She sat down at Garrett's desk and pulled open the top drawer. Inside, she saw a small stack of plain white postcards.

Before she could have time for second thoughts,

she penned a short note to her father. Then she added a stamp and ran the card out to the mailbox. Garrett had already placed his outgoing mail in the box, so she knew he wouldn't see it and question her about it.

Back in the bedroom, she changed into her night-shirt and burrowed under the covers. She wanted to read more of the journal, but exhaustion overcame her. Shortly after her head hit the pillow, she fell fast asleep.

And dreamed about kissing Garrett Lord behind a hog shed.

GARRETT HAD one chance left.

If he didn't want to spend the next four weeks fighting his feelings for Mimi, he had to find a way to make her leave. Today.

She walked into the kitchen, her blond hair pulled into a sassy ponytail and a wide smile on those delectable lips. "Isn't it a beautiful morning?"

Garrett looked up from his third cup of coffee, wondering where he'd gone wrong. After staying up half the night, Mimi looked better today than the day she'd arrived. His eyelids felt like sandpaper every time he blinked, and he'd been yawning practically nonstop since his alarm clock had gone off at six.

"Mmm, that coffee smells delicious." She moved toward the counter and poured herself a steaming cup. Then she turned to face him. "So what's on the agenda today, boss?"

"Chores first," he said, setting his fork on his plate. "Then we'll check the cows. After that…" He hesitated, wondering if he was playing fair. Mimi might be a city girl, but she'd shown spunk and determination he'd rarely seen in a woman. Truth be told, she was turning into a hell of a fine ranch hand, even if she did have a few unorthodox methods. Like herding cattle with cow pies.

She sat across from him and picked up a piece of buttered toast. "Don't keep me in suspense."

He looked into her sky-blue eyes and experienced the same odd reaction he'd had outside the corral. She was just so damn enticing. He'd almost blown it last night. Almost kissed her again. And that definitely wasn't in her job description. Hell, he'd be lucky if she didn't sue him for sexual harassment.

It was time to send Mimi home, before he gave in to these ridiculous urges. Before he did something he was sure to regret.

"After we check the cows," he said, taking a deep breath and plunging ahead before he could change his mind, "we're going to do some target practice in the canyon."

She paled. "Target practice. As in guns?"

"That's right. You know how to shoot a rifle, don't you?"

"Actually, no. Maybe I should just stay here and…keep an eye on the cows."

He shook his head. "Every ranch hand needs to know how to handle a rifle. You'll have to ride Flint today. Pooh isn't used to the sound of gunfire."

From the disgruntled expression on her face, neither was Mimi. Garrett ignored the way his conscience pricked at him the rest of the morning. Clearing predators off the place was part of a ranch hand's duties.

If Mimi couldn't handle the job, then she didn't belong here. It was pure and simple.

His resolve began to waver three hours later as they rode their horses single file into the canyon just south of the ranch. She looked pale on her horse, a huge gray gelding Garrett had assured her wouldn't bolt at the sound of gunfire or at the sight of a rattlesnake.

He wished he could be as certain about her.

But I want her to bolt, he reminded himself. *All the way back to Austin.*

Garrett reined in his horse and waited for Mimi to catch up with him.

Her gaze traveled slowly over the canyon. "I don't see any rattlesnakes."

"It's a good thing," he said, climbing from his horse and looping the reins around the stump of a mesquite tree, "since you don't know how to shoot yet."

She stayed astride Flint. "Did I mention I don't like guns? That I've never even touched a gun before?"

He checked the barrel of the rifle just to make sure it was empty. "It's part of the job, Mimi. Take it or leave it."

Mimi bit her bottom lip, obviously considering her options. Garrett's heart began to pound hard in his chest as he awaited her decision. Which was odd, since he didn't have anything at stake except his peace of mind.

"I'll take it," she said quietly, then dropped down off her horse. After hitching it to the same mesquite tree, she took the rifle out of his hands.

"You sure you want to do this?" he asked.

"No." The rifle shook slightly in her hands, but

her gaze didn't waver from his face. "But I'm sure I want to stay on as your ranch hand, so I'll do whatever is necessary."

He folded his arms across his chest. "Why?"

She hesitated. "Because it's important to me. I set out to prove to you that I'm more than just some fluffy city girl. But now I want to prove it to myself. If I have to shoot a few rattlesnakes to do it, then...I will."

He'd lost, and he knew it, but he couldn't back down now. The way her hands were shaking, she'd be lucky to hit the side of the canyon. "Okay. Time for your first lesson."

She perched the butt of the rifle against her shoulder. "I'm ready."

"Good. Now put the rifle down."

She lowered the barrel until it touched the ground, then frowned at him. "I thought you wanted me to learn to shoot."

"I do. But the most important part of learning to shoot is making sure you don't shoot yourself. Or me." He leaned forward and pointed near the trigger. "This is the safety switch. Always make sure it's on before you pick up any gun. Once it's in position, the trigger will not engage." He demonstrated for her, then had her try it for herself.

"Okay," she said, "the safety is on."

"Now you need to see if the rifle is loaded." He took the rifle from her hands, then pumped it once. "This is the chamber."

She peered into it. "Looks empty to me."

"Right. But that's no guarantee. Pump it at least

three more times just to make certain. If there is a bullet in there, it won't pump."

Her blond brows drew together. "This all sounds extremely complicated. When do I get to shoot something?"

He handed her the rifle. "Okay, the safety is on and the chamber is empty. Now it's time to lock and load."

He showed her how to place a rifle shell in the chamber and lock it into place. "Aim for that juniper tree over there."

She placed the butt of the rifle against her shoulder, then cracked one eye open as she looked down the barrel of the gun. "Now what do I do?"

"Gently squeeze the trigger. And be ready for—" His words were drowned out as the shell exploded from the rifle. The recoil sent Mimi flying backward. She landed with a hard thud right on her rear end.

He bit back a smile as he helped her to her feet. "I tried to warn you about that."

"You could have said something sooner," she sputtered, wiping dirt and sage grass off the back of her jeans. Then she reached up to rub her shoulder. "That hurt."

"You just have to be prepared for it next time."

She peered at her target. "Did I hit the tree?"

"Not quite. Next time, don't close both eyes when you pull the trigger. Hold the butt of the rifle tightly against your shoulder and brace your feet with your left leg slightly out in front."

"How?"

"Like this." He came up behind her, wrapping his arms around her so he could place the rifle in the correct position on her shoulder. He could smell her hair and the faint, earthy scent of perspiration on her neck. Her body leaned slightly into his as she adjusted her footing. Garrett bit down hard on the inside of his cheek, attempting to remain immune to her nearness. And failing miserably.

"Okay, I think I'm ready," she said.

Garrett stepped back, his heart beating an erratic tattoo in his chest. He watched Mimi turn on the safety switch, check the chamber, then lock and load. Clenching her jaw, she took careful aim at the juniper tree and cracked one eye open. Then she fired.

Garrett's jaw dropped in disbelief as one of the branches exploded off the tree.

"I did it!" This time the recoil of the rifle had backed her up a couple steps, but she'd managed to stay on her feet. "Did you see that, Garrett?"

"I sure did." He handed her another shell. "Now let's see if it was just a lucky shot."

She missed the next two, but connected on the third.

The shooting lesson continued long into the afternoon. At last they stopped to lunch on the tuna salad sandwiches Mimi had prepared. He almost could have enjoyed their impromptu picnic if he didn't feel so sneaky. Mimi was thrilled with her shooting success and anxious to try more target practice. Only she didn't know the kind of shooting he had in mind.

"I want to aim for something smaller now," she said, licking bread crumbs off her fingers. She rose to her feet and reached for the rifle.

He was about to suggest shooting at a stunted shrub

when his intended prey came into target. Much sooner than he'd expected.

"Is something wrong?" she asked as he rose slowly and carefully to his feet.

He nodded toward the small outcropping of rocks just to the east of them. "Look over there. A coyote."

Her gaze finally caught sight of the small coyote, still oblivious to their presence.

"He's beautiful," she breathed.

Garrett thought the critter just looked mangy and scrawny. But then his opinion was probably colored by the fact that coyotes like this one killed a number of his calves every season. "Shoot him."

She gaped at him. "What?"

"He's a predator, Mimi. If you don't shoot him, he may kill that calf we watched come into the world last night." He handed her a rifle shell.

She stared at it as if she'd never seen one before. Then she slowly loaded it into the rifle.

"Quiet now," he whispered as she pumped the rifle. "You don't want to run him off."

Mimi perched the rifle on her shoulder, her face pale and drawn. Something in her blue eyes made Garrett's stomach give a sickening lurch. He opened his mouth to stop her when the rifle exploded. He whirled to look at the coyote.

The shot flew clear over its head, but the coyote didn't stick around to give her another chance. It scampered behind the rocks and out of sight.

Garrett turned to face Mimi. Tears shimmered in her eyes as she held the rifle toward him. "I missed."

"Don't worry about it," he said, taking the rifle from her. "It was a tough shot."

"You don't understand, Garrett. I missed on purpose." She spun on her heel and strode toward her horse. It only took her a few seconds to untie the reins and mount up.

"Mimi, wait," he said, regret churning in his gut.

"Looks like you were right," she said, her hands gripping the reins. "I don't belong here."

He watched her ride off toward the ranch. Another wave of guilt washed over him even as he tried to rationalize his actions. Shooting coyotes was part of a ranch hand's job, he told himself as he gathered the rifle and the remains of their lunch. Though he had to admit he'd never actually shot one unless it was in the act of threatening his cattle.

Still, they'd made a deal, and she hadn't kept her end of the bargain. It would be better for both of them if she went back to Austin.

He kept repeating that to himself on the long journey to the ranch. He almost believed it by the time he reached the barn.

Then he heard her scream.

CHAPTER SEVEN

GARRETT FOUND HER in the tack room. She lay unmoving on the floor, clutching her right wrist. Her
face shone a pasty white, and her lips were bloodless
and clenched with pain.

"Mimi?" He rushed into the room and knelt beside
her. "What's wrong? Did you fall?"

She shook her head. "No." Then she squeezed her
eyes shut. "It hurts so much."

His gaze moved to her wrist. Her left hand was still
wrapped tightly around it, so he couldn't tell if it was
cut or broken. "Let me see it," he said, gently prying
her fingers off her wrist.

She flinched at his touch, her eyes wet with tears.
"Please don't touch me."

His heart contracted at the pain in her voice.
"Mimi, I can't help you unless I see what's wrong."

"It was a scorpion. It stung me."

Cold fear enveloped him. "What color was it?"

She licked her dry lips. "Yellow. With little brown
stripes."

A striped bark scorpion. Garrett told himself not to
panic. The sting of a scorpion could be deadly, but
only for those extremely allergic. "Have you ever
been stung by a scorpion before?"

She shook her head. "It hurts like hell."

"I know." He looked from her pale face to her wrist. "Maybe we should go to the hospital."

"No." She inhaled a deep, shaky breath. "I'm fine. Besides, I hate hospitals. Too much…blood."

Too concerned to argue, he scooped her up in his arms and carried her out of the tack room. She felt weightless in his arms, and he had to keep himself from running with her toward the house. He'd had a friend from high school who had been stung by a scorpion before football practice one day. It had crawled into his jersey and stung him twice on the back while he was dressing for a game.

Kevin had almost died from that sting.

Garrett managed to turn the knob on the front door, then kicked it open all the way. Fine drops of perspiration dotted Mimi's forehead.

He tried not to remember that Kevin's first symptom had been heavy sweating. Followed by blurred vision and difficulty swallowing.

He laid her gently on the sofa, then covered her from neck to toe with the lonestar quilt.

"My boots are filthy," she protested, still clutching her wrist.

"Don't worry about it," he said, amazed she could be concerned about something as inconsequential as dirty boots when she might be… No. He wouldn't let himself even think of that possibility. "I'll be right back."

He dashed into the kitchen, made a quick phone call, then scooped ice out of the freezer and into a large bowl. He carried the bowl into the living room. "How do you feel?"

"Like a fool," she replied, a faint blush on her

cheeks. Or was the redness there due to the sting? He laid a hand on her forehead. "You feel warm."

"That's because I just spent all afternoon out in the sun. I'm fine, Garrett. Really."

She did seem fine, but he wasn't about to take any chances. He placed the bowl of ice beside her on the sofa. "Put your wrist in here. It will help ease the pain."

Grimacing, she carefully lowered her hand into the ice.

He could see the sting mark, raw and red on the inside of her wrist. They sat there silently for the next fifteen minutes or so.

"That does feel better," she said at last, relaxing her shoulders against the sofa cushion.

His panic began to ebb. "How did it happen?"

"It was my own fault," she said, staring at the ceiling. "I found something in the north wall of the tack room yesterday. An old journal. I thought there might be other treasures hidden back there, as well, so I reached my hand underneath the gap in the floorboard." She shook her head in disgust. "I found something, all right. Or should I say, it found me."

"Don't ever do anything like that again," he said, sounding more gruff than he intended. He could still hear her scream in his mind. Still remember how the sound had ripped him apart inside. He never wanted to feel that way again.

"I don't think you have to worry about it," she said softly. "I'll be leaving today."

"You're not going anywhere." He said the words before he had time to consider them. But once they were out, he didn't try to take them back.

"I have to leave," she persisted. "I couldn't shoot the coyote. Which means I couldn't live up to my end of the bargain. But I want to thank you, Garrett, for giving me a chance."

"Don't thank me," he rasped. Then he stood and started pacing back and forth across the hardwood floor.

"Is something wrong?"

He stopped to face her. "Do you want to leave?"

"No, but—"

"Then you're staying," he interjected. "It's too late for me to find another ranch hand, anyway. By the time I contact the employment agency and conduct interviews, calving season will be half over."

She narrowed her eyes. "I don't want you to let me stay because you feel sorry for me."

"The last thing I feel for you is sorry." He raked one hand through his hair, trying to figure out his feelings himself. Attraction was at the top of the list. But he also felt respect. And curiosity. What would make a city girl so anxious to leave everything familiar behind her?

Or maybe the question should be *who?*

A knock at the door interrupted his musings.

Mimi's brows drew together. "Are you expecting someone?"

"I sure am." He strode to the door and opened it, relief flowing through him when he saw the woman who stood on the other side. The only doctor he could impose on to make a house call. "Thank God you're here, Abby."

"Where is she?" Abby asked, reaching out to give his forearm a gentle, reassuring squeeze.

He nodded toward the living room. "On the sofa."

He ushered Abby into the house, her calm, collected manner already making him feel better. He'd known her forever. The Maitland and Lord children had grown up like cousins. Abby had always been a little on the serious side, but he liked that about her. He liked her new husband, Kyle McDermott, too. Their marriage had put a sparkle in Abby's eyes that had never been there before.

"Are you a doctor?" Mimi asked, struggling to sit up on the sofa.

"Actually, I'm an obstetrician-gynecologist at the Maitland Maternity Clinic," Abby said, placing one hand on Mimi's shoulder. "Lie down now, and let me have a look at you."

Mimi stared at Garrett. "You sent for an obstetrician?"

"I wanted you to see a doctor, and Abby was available," he explained.

"He told me you were in trouble." Abby reached for Mimi's uninjured arm to feel her pulse.

"Not *that* kind of trouble," Mimi exclaimed.

Abby looked at him and laughed. "You're blushing, Garrett."

He cleared his throat, annoyed to feel the heat in his cheeks. "It's hot in here."

Abby looked between the two of them, a smile playing on her lips. "It certainly is."

"Have a seat, Abby," he said, moving a chair closer to the sofa.

Abby sat down, giving Mimi her full attention. "Now, Garrett told me you were stung by a scorpion.

Let's have a look." She gently removed Mimi's hand from the bowl of ice. "Is it painful?"

"It was at first, but it's not so much anymore. The ice really helped."

"Good." Abby tenderly prodded the skin around the reddened sting with one finger. "How about other symptoms? Do you have any difficulty swallowing or breathing?"

Mimi shook her head. "No. I feel fine. Just a little shaky."

Abby nodded. "I think that's normal under the circumstances."

Garrett fisted his hands at his sides. Mimi still looked incredibly pale to him. "I think she got stung by a striped bark scorpion."

"Ouch," Abby replied, opening her medical bag. "Those nasty things definitely hurt. I've got some antibiotic cream I'd like you to rub on the wound every couple of hours. It should help decrease the pain and swelling, too."

"Anything else?" Garrett asked, taking the tube of salve from her hands before Mimi could reach for it.

"Just some aspirin and bed rest. You can call me if she starts to experience any of the symptoms I mentioned, but I strongly doubt that will happen now."

Mimi wiggled her sore hand back into the bowl of ice. "Can I ask you a question, Dr....?"

"Please call me Abby."

"Okay...Abby. Since when do doctors make house calls?"

Abby smiled. "Garrett's just lucky he caught me between deliveries. But he knows I'd do just about anything for him, including a house call or two."

Mimi laid her head back on the sofa cushion.

"Sounds like he's lucky to know you."

"The Maitlands are lucky to know him," Abby countered, gazing at him. "Especially my brother Jake. Garrett took a bullet that was meant for him."

Garrett stepped forward before Abby could embarrass him further. "Thanks for coming, Abby."

She snapped her bag closed and stood up. "Any time, Garrett. Walk me to the door?"

He tucked the quilt around Mimi's shoulders, then escorted Abby out the front door and onto the porch. "I appreciate you coming out here so fast, Abby. I was really worried there for a while."

"I know," she said gently. "I'm glad I could help."

He hesitated, rubbing a rough spot on the porch rail with his thumb. "Are you sure she'll be all right?"

"She'll be fine." Abby smiled. "Although maybe I should write her a prescription."

He recognized the teasing note in her voice. "What for?"

"Birth control." Abby's smile widened into a grin. "From the way you look at her, I'd say she's going to need it."

IT SEEMED LIKE forever until Garrett walked into the house. Mimi had been struggling to stay awake, her curiosity overcoming her exhaustion.

Garrett walked toward her, a frown on his handsome face. "Why did you take your hand out of the ice?"

"Because it was turning into an ice cube. Besides, it feels much better now. Really."

He picked up the half-melted bowl of ice and headed for the kitchen. A few moments later, he returned with a glass of water and two aspirins.

"Here," he said, handing her the pills. "Take these, and then I want you to get some rest."

She popped the pills into her mouth, then washed them down with the water. "Are you going to tell me a bedtime story?"

He looked chagrined. "I don't know any."

"How about telling me exactly what Abby meant about you taking a bullet for her brother."

Garrett sat in the chair beside the sofa. "I don't think that kind of story is going to put you to sleep."

"Tell me anyway." Her blue eyes softened with concern. "I want to know."

He sighed, then leaned forward in the chair, his elbows propped on his knees. "Jake Maitland is a good friend of mine. A woman he knew was in trouble, and he asked if she could stay out here for a while until things cooled off."

"What kind of trouble?"

"An ex-husband who didn't want to let her go."

Mimi shifted on the sofa, wincing slightly at the movement. "Is he the one who shot you?"

Garrett nodded. "The bullet didn't do any serious damage."

She scowled at him. "Anytime you get shot is serious, Garrett. Where did it hit you?"

Without a word, he began unbuttoning his shirt. Despite her exhaustion and the tingling pain in her wrist, a frisson of excitement zipped through her veins as his fingers undid each button. His shirt gapped open to reveal dark russet hair on his broad chest. When he pulled the tails of his shirt out of his jeans, she saw the ripple of washboard muscles above his waist and swallowed convulsively.

"See," he said, pointing to a silvery scar on his left shoulder, just above his heart. "It's hardly even noticeable anymore."

She reached out her left hand to trace the long, narrow scar with one finger. His skin contracted at her touch, and she heard the breath catch in his throat.

"Does that hurt?"

"No." He leaned away from her and began to button his shirt.

"I'm glad you're all right."

The tension in his face eased. "Me, too." He stood up. "Are you ready for bed now?"

She nodded, then swung her legs over the sofa to stand up. But Garrett didn't give her a chance. He swept her into his arms, quilt and all.

She sighed and laid her head on his shoulder. "You know, this is really getting to be a bad habit. I'm perfectly capable of walking."

"I just don't want to take any chances."

Mimi closed her eyes as he carried her into her bedroom, letting herself imagine that he was taking her there for an entirely different reason. Her heart skittered in her chest at the thought of Garrett joining her in bed.

She opened her eyes as he lowered her gently to the mattress. "Thanks for the ride."

"Any time," he said huskily, then drew the bedclothes over her. "Now, go to sleep."

She dutifully closed her eyes, aware that Garrett still stood over her. Breathing deeply, she could smell the faint aroma of his musky aftershave. Feeling sleepy and snug under the blankets, she let herself drift into the delicious fantasy that had formed in her mind just moments ago.

When Garrett's lips brushed her mouth, she smiled. It was the best dream she'd had in a very long time.

"WAKE UP, sleepyhead."

Mimi opened her eyes and automatically looked at the clock on her bed stand. "Eight o'clock? Why did you let me sleep so late? I should have done chores two hours ago!"

She threw off the bedclothes, but Garrett pushed her down onto the pillows and drew the blanket over her. "Relax. It's eight o'clock at night, not morning. You've been sleeping for the last five hours, but I didn't want you to miss supper."

"Oh." She blinked and sat up in bed, still slightly disoriented. A dull ache in her wrist brought everything rushing back. The scorpion sting. Abby's visit. Garrett's kiss. Or had that last event really happened?

"What's wrong?" he said, pulling up a chair beside the bed. "You look confused."

She shook her head. "I'm fine. Just a little woozy."

"Maybe this will help." He reached behind him and lifted a bed tray off the dresser. Mimi's mouth watered as he set the tray in front of her, steam rising from the big bowl of soup in the center of it.

"Is this what I think it is?"

"Chicken soup," he affirmed. "It cures everything from scorpion stings to—"

"Bullet wounds," she interjected, then picked up

the spoon. "I take it you used this tray a time or two after you were shot?"

He nodded. "My sisters took turns coddling me for much longer than was necessary. Chicken soup is one of Shelby's specialties. She left about twenty gallons of it in the freezer for me."

She took her first bite. "It's delicious. Tell Shelby she's a great cook."

"You can tell her yourself."

Mimi looked at him, her spoon poised in midair. "Is she here?"

"No, but you'll probably see her Saturday night at Connor O'Hara's barbecue."

"Thanks, but I doubt anyone expects you to bring your ranch hand along to the party."

A muscle flickered in his check. "No, but I can definitely bring a date."

Mimi kept her gaze on the soup bowl, willing herself not to read too much into his invitation. "Are you sure Venna won't mind? She told me...." Her voice trailed off as she remembered how Garrett had reacted the last time she'd brought up the subject of Venna.

"This isn't about Venna. This is about you and me." He stared at her for a long moment. "Look, I'm not trying to put you on the spot. I realize you're an engaged woman. If you'd rather not go to the party with me..."

"I'm not engaged anymore," she said, before he had a chance to retract his invitation. "And I'd love to go. Thank you for asking me."

"Eat your soup," he said gruffly, leaning back in his chair.

She finished every last drop, then settled against the

pillows. The warm glow inside her had nothing to do with chicken soup and everything to do with Garrett asking her on a date. "Can I get up now?"

He scowled. "Absolutely not. The doctor ordered complete bed rest."

"But—"

"No buts. If you stay in bed the rest of the night, I *might* let you get up tomorrow."

She frowned. "Were your sisters this bossy when you were the patient?"

"Worse," he replied, setting the bed tray on the dresser. "Now I want you to try to get some more sleep."

She rolled her eyes. "I just slept for five hours straight and I don't feel the least bit sleepy. How about another bedtime story?"

"I'm fresh out."

"I'm not." She reached over to the bedstand, opened the top drawer, then drew out the old journal and handed it to him.

"What's this?" he said, turning it over in his hand.

"The buried treasure I found in your tack room."

He opened the journal, then whistled low. "Eighteen ninety-eight? I knew that barn was old, but I didn't realize it was that old."

Mimi snuggled down under the blankets, savoring the warmth and the odd sensation that she and Garrett were the only two people on the earth. Her hand still ached slightly, but she could put up with a little pain to stay on the ranch. To stay with Garrett.

He cracked open the journal. "Where should I start?"

"The last entry I read was dated December fifth, so start at the one after that."

He flipped through the pages, then leaned back in his chair and began reading.

December 7, 1898
That nosy Minnie Jo spied me and Boyd kissing. I had to give her my best hair ribbon to keep her from telling Mama. Mama doesn't like him because he won't come to church. But Pa says a man can worship God just as well on the wide open range as he can on a hard church pew. When I asked Boyd if he prays on the range, he said he's been praying every day that I'll let him kiss me again.

"Kiss him again?" Garrett began paging back through the journal. "What exactly have I missed?"

"Katherine is falling for her father's new ranch hand, Boyd Harrison," Mimi informed him. "He kissed her behind the hog shed."

"Sounds like Boyd isn't wasting any time."

"I think she's falling in love with him." Mimi knew firsthand how hard it was to resist a handsome cowboy.

"She's only…what?" He flipped to the first entry of the journal. "Eighteen? That's much too young to fall in love."

She smiled. "I didn't realize there was a minimum age requirement."

"Well, there should be if girls like Katherine let some traveling cowboy lure them behind a hog shed.

And it sounds like good old Boyd is going to find himself on the wrong end of a shotgun if her father finds out.''

Mimi turned on her side to face him. "We won't find out unless you keep reading."

Garrett thumbed through the pages until he found the next entry.

December 12, 1898
I used up almost all my egg money to buy some beautiful blue linen fabric at the mercantile today in Austin. It's the same color as Boyd's eyes. I told him I'd make him three fine handkerchiefs and sew his initials on them. When I asked him to tell me his middle name, he told me it begins with S, but I must guess it. I guessed Samuel, Silas, Simon, Saul, Sebastian, and Sherman. He laughed the hardest when I guessed Sassafras. I'll sew BSH on the handkerchiefs, but I won't give up until I learn his middle name. I want to know everything about him. He's on my mind when I go to sleep at night and when I wake up in the morning. I wish Mama liked him so I could ask her if this is love.

Garrett looked up from the journal. "I think the S stands for smooth talker."

"Keep reading," Mimi ordered, dismayed to find her eyelids growing heavy.

December 24, 1898
I finished the handkerchiefs and wrapped them with a pretty red bow I've saved for a special

occasion. Since only Minnie Jo knows about Boyd and me, I had to sneak off to the barn after the folks went to bed. There was a full moon and it was so romantic in the hayloft, just Boyd and me.

He told me he has a hankering to build a ranch down near San Antonio. Then he asked me if I'd go all that way with him. Of course, I said yes! He didn't exactly propose, but my heart started pounding so fast I couldn't hardly breathe. This is the most romantic thing that has ever happened to me.

Oh, if only I could tell Mama! She married Pa when she was only seventeen, a year younger than me, so she should understand true love. But she's dead set against Boyd. I don't understand how she can hate him so much.

I love him with all my heart.

When Mimi opened her eyes, Garrett was gone and all the lights were out. She leaned over to look at the clock on the bed stand, surprised to find it was after midnight. Realizing she must have fallen asleep again, Mimi got out of bed and quickly changed out of her work clothes and into one of Garrett's old T-shirts that she'd been using as a nightshirt.

She walked to the window and leaned her head against the cool windowpane. The moon hung low in the clear night sky, and a canopy of stars twinkled at her. Mimi wrapped her arms around herself, the edge of the T-shirt whispering against her thighs. It seemed odd to think that Katherine had stared at the same moon, perhaps on a night just like this. Had her life been filled with more joy or sorrow?

Mimi knew it was time to make some decisions about her own life. In a few short weeks, her sojourn on this ranch would come to an end. Then it would be time to face her father. And Paul.

She suppressed a shiver, then padded back to the bed, pulling the warm blankets around her shoulders. Austin and all her problems seemed very far away at the moment.

But she couldn't hide from them forever.

CHAPTER EIGHT

THE SHRILL RING of the telephone woke Paul Renquist from a restless sleep. He fumbled for the receiver, then picked it up. "Hello?"

"This is Harper. You awake?"

"I am now," he growled.

"Good. We need to talk."

Paul sat up in bed. "You found her?"

"Not yet, but I did find Rupert Casville in my office today."

"Shit." A dull, throbbing ache began in Paul's left temple.

"Daddy Casville got a postcard from his daughter. Want me to read it to you?"

"Of course," he snapped.

"'Dad, I'm fine,'" Harper read over the phone. "'Please don't worry about me. And don't forget to take your medicine. Love, Mimi.'"

Paul took a deep breath. "Where is she?"

"According to the postmark, she was still in Austin as of yesterday. But there's no return address."

"What was Rupert's reaction?" he asked, wondering why the old man hadn't informed him of this latest development. It gave him a queasy, uneasy feeling in the pit of his stomach.

"Relief, mostly," Harper replied. "In fact, he's

certain Mimi will be home soon. So certain that he
fired me.''

"So let him think you're off the case," Paul replied, irritated by the whine in Harper's voice. "I'm
paying you more than enough money to stay on it.''

Harper blew into the phone. "Look, Renquist, I
don't much like double-crossing Casville. If he finds
out, he could ruin me.''

Paul pinched the bridge of his nose between his
fingers. The last thing he wanted to do at two o'clock
in the morning was baby-sit a chicken-shit private in-
vestigator.

"Hey, Paul? You still there?''

Paul sighed. "I told you the old man is sick. The
doctor put him on some new kind of medication that
makes him irrational. Just leave everything to me.''

"Cut the crap. We both know you're setting Casville up for some kind of scam. Why else would you
want dirt on his daughter?''

"I have my reasons.''

"Hey, don't get me wrong," Harper said with a
low chuckle. "It takes guts to pull one past the old
man. In fact, I admire you so much, I'm willing to
stay on the job for a cool hundred grand.''

"That's bullshit!''

"Think again, Paulie." Harper sounded calm, almost as if he was enjoying himself. "I'm the one
doing all the legwork here.''

"You haven't found Mimi," Paul exclaimed. "You
haven't done a damn thing to earn one lousy dime!
How hard can it be to locate a woman in a wedding
dress?''

"Don't tell me how to do my job," Harper

snapped. "I'll find her. Especially now that I know she's still in Austin. I just need a little more time."

Paul raked one hand through his rumpled hair. "Exactly how much time? I expected to be on my honeymoon by now."

"Hey, I just said I'll find her. But I can't make her marry you."

"Let me worry about that."

"Fine. Why don't you worry about this, too. If Casville finds out you're directly defying his orders, he'll cut you off at the knees."

Paul closed his eyes against the pain in his head. "Is that a threat?"

The jerk was scamming him. Maybe Harper had found Mimi already and was just stringing him along to get more money. He was tempted to slam down the phone. But he hadn't gotten this far in life by losing control of his temper. He'd play the game and come out on top.

Just like he always did.

"Look, I've kept my mouth shut." Harper let the moment linger. "So far."

Paul licked his lips, his headache evolving into one of his rare migraines. "Okay. I'll give you an extra twenty thousand."

"It's too late at night to make jokes, Paul. Try again."

"Twenty-five."

"I've got Daddy Casville's phone number right in front of me, and my dialing finger is starting to itch."

Paul stared out the huge picture window of his luxury penthouse apartment, the lights of Austin blurring as the pain in his head increased. "All right. But fifty is as high as I'll go."

"You took so long, my price went up. Now I want sixty grand."

Paul's hand curled tightly around the telephone receiver. He wished it was Harper's scrawny neck. "Deal."

"Good. When do I get my money?"

"When you find Mimi. But I want to be the one who supervises the happy reunion. So you don't get a dime if she suddenly shows up on Daddy's doorstep."

"That won't happen," Harper replied. "I guarantee it."

THE O'HARAS' BARBECUE was already in full swing by the time Mimi and Garrett arrived. A local country band played on a makeshift stage set up in front of the horse paddock. The savory aroma of sizzling beef emanated from the barbecue pit in the center of the yard. Garrett and Mimi waited in a receiving line in front of Connor and Lacy O'Hara's sprawling house.

Garrett leaned toward Mimi's ear. "Did I mention you look wonderful tonight?"

She smiled at him. "Only about five times."

"Is that all? Then I'll say it again. You look wonderful."

"Thank you." She let her gaze travel slowly over his snug black denim jeans and neatly pressed charcoal shirt. "You don't look half bad yourself."

Garrett lightly placed his hand on her back and propelled her forward. His touch sent a tingle straight down to her toes. She was as giddy as a girl on her first date, though she'd never been to a party like this before. When the Casvilles and their society friends entertained, no one wore blue jeans or cowboy hats. They dined on pâté and truffles. Danced to a string quartet instead of cowboy music. And basically bored each other to death.

But tonight she wasn't Mimi Casville, daughter of one of the richest men in Texas. She was Mimi Banyon, ranch hand. Complete with a new outfit for her Saturday night date. Garrett had finally convinced her to accept an advance on her wages, so she'd driven his pickup to a store on the outskirts of Austin that carried farm supplies and Western wear. That's where she'd found the cream silk blouse and wheat-colored denim jeans. Not her usual style, but Mimi liked the look.

And from the way her date kept staring at her, he did, too.

Garrett clasped her hand in his as they worked their way through the crowd. She'd already been introduced to every one of the Maitlands and was still trying to keep them all straight in her head.

Lacy O'Hara was sweet, and much younger than Connor, her handsome husband. But you could tell by the way they looked at each other that their love was timeless.

Abby was there, and insisted on examining Mimi's wrist, the sting barely visible now. Then Abby introduced her husband, Kyle McDermott. Mimi had panicked for a moment, recognizing him as one of her father's business associates. But Kyle didn't seem to make any connection. Mimi soon relaxed, realizing he was too entranced by his wife to give her a second glance.

The rest of the Maitlands seemed very fond of Garrett, and he obviously returned their affection. Mimi could see that despite his early abandonment, there were plenty of people who loved her boss.

She watched him as he stopped to talk with Jake Maitland, and wondered if Garrett realized how rich he really was. Her financial future was more than secure, and her bank account full to bursting, but was there anyone alive who loved her unconditionally?

The sound of Garrett's deep laugh shook her out of her maudlin reverie. She'd never been one to give in to self-pity and wasn't about to start now. Especially on such a beautiful, balmy night.

Garrett caught her gaze and held it as he carried on a conversation with Jake. Something in his eyes made her breath come quicker. It was the oddest feeling. Even though they were standing several feet apart, she felt close to him—connected in some odd way.

At last, Jake's wife, Camille, walked up and laughingly pulled her husband away. Mimi smiled as Garrett approached, then she saw him frown as he looked over her shoulder.

"Uh-oh," he muttered. "I think it's too late to hide."

Mimi turned to see another one of Garrett's admirers scurrying over to them. Only this one could almost be classified as a stalker.

"There you are!" Venna flashed a wide smile at Mimi's date. "I've been looking everywhere for you, Garrett Lord."

"Evening, Venna. You remember Mimi?" He turned and slid his arm around Mimi's waist.

"Of course." Venna's smile dimmed. "How are you?"

"Fine, thank you." Mimi was more confused than ever by the woman's behavior. At their last visit, Venna had implied that she and Garrett were an item. Yet she didn't act hurt or offended that he'd shown up with a date.

Venna turned her attention to Garrett. "My, my, you do clean up good, Garrett Lord. In fact, you look good enough to eat."

A young woman with auburn hair appeared next to Venna. "My brother would give you indigestion, Venna. You'd better stick to barbecue."

Garrett grinned. "Hey, Lana. Is that any way to talk about your big brother?"

She circled one arm around his waist and gave him an affectionate squeeze. "Somebody has to protect you."

"Speaking of protection," he said, returning the hug, "where's that new husband of yours? I'm surprised he let you out of his sight."

She hitched her thumb over her shoulder. "He's in the stable showing our son the new foal."

"Please excuse me," Venna said. "I have to go see if Lacy needs any help in the kitchen." Then she gave him a jaunty wave. "Save me a dance, Garrett."

Lana watched her walk away, then turned and arched one auburn brow. "I'm surprised you showed up here tonight, Garrett."

"I never miss a good barbecue," he replied, clearing his throat. "This is my date, Mimi Banyon. Mimi, this is my kid sister, Lana Van Zandt."

"It's a pleasure to meet you," Mimi said, noting the striking resemblance between Garrett and his sister, although Lana's complexion was much fairer than Garrett's.

"It's wonderful to meet you," Lana replied, clasping Mimi's hand in her own. "I can't remember the last time my brother was out on a date."

"Lana," Garrett admonished under his breath.

She clapped a hand over her mouth, but Mimi could still see the smile she wasn't trying very hard to hide. "Whoops. Me and my big mouth. Seems like it gets me into trouble all the time."

"Maybe you should fill it up with some food," Garrett suggested.

"Good idea. Why don't you go get some barbecue for all of us while Mimi and I find a place to sit?"

Garrett started to refuse, then shook his head in defeat and walked toward the barbecue line.

"I want a double serving of coleslaw," Lana yelled after him.

Mimi couldn't help but like Garrett's sister. Even when she turned into an amateur private eye.

"Okay," Lana said, once they were alone. "Tell me everything."

"What exactly do you want to know?" Mimi asked as they walked to an empty picnic table and sat down.

"Well, for starters, how did you and my brother meet?"

"He found me in his hayloft. One thing led to another, and now I'm Garrett's new ranch hand. At least until calving season is over."

Lana's eyes widened. "Sounds like you're leaving a few good parts out of your story."

"Maybe just a few." Mimi smiled. "You'll have to ask your brother to tell you the rest."

"I'll definitely do that." Lana glanced at Venna. "Just between you and me, I'm surprised she's taking all of this so calmly."

"Me, too." Mimi lowered her voice a notch. "Especially since Venna told me Garrett asked her to marry him."

Lana laughed. "Did she also happen to mention that this marriage proposal took place several years ago?"

A feeling oddly like relief flowed through her. "No."

"Venna and my brother had one of those summertime flings when he first started working at his ranch. Of course, it wasn't his yet, he'd hired on as one of the hands. Anyway, she flirted outrageously with him, and he was still young enough to be flattered by all the attention. But it didn't last."

"They broke it off?"

"Not exactly." Lana's gaze wavered, then she leaned forward. "I know Garrett will probably kill me for telling you this, but Venna left him at the altar."

Mimi's stomach twisted into a tight knot at her words. "Oh, no."

"Well, not literally," Lana amended. "She took off the night before the wedding. But she didn't bother to tell Garrett, or even leave him a note. He didn't find out until he got to the church. Her father's ranch foreman told him."

No wonder he'd reacted so oddly to her story the

night she'd met him. He'd once been in the shoes of the groom. "Poor Garrett."

"Don't ever let him hear you say that," Lana admonished. "Besides, he's thanked his lucky stars more than once for that narrow escape."

"Are you sure? Venna is a beautiful woman."

"She's also been rueing the day she ran away from him. It took two bad marriages to make her realize what she gave up."

"And now she wants him back," Mimi mused.

"That's right. But let me tell you something about my brother, Mimi. He doesn't forgive or forget. Venna can chase him from here to Kalamazoo, and he'll never give her a second chance. Once you've broken Garrett's trust, or his heart, you'll never get either one back."

"That sounds like a warning," Mimi said softly.

Lana smiled. "Just a little friendly advice. I love my brother and I want to see him happy. Of course, it would help if he wasn't so stubborn about *everything.*"

Mimi couldn't help but laugh at the note of frustration she heard in Lana's voice. She'd felt that same frustration herself a time or two, and she'd only known him a week.

"Dinner is served," Garrett announced, approaching the picnic table with three fully loaded plates balanced in his big hands.

Mimi grabbed one of the plates, a dollop of thick barbecue sauce dripping onto her thumb. She sucked it off, savoring the tangy flavor. Then she looked up to see Garrett staring at her, his gaze fixed on her mouth. Her skin tingled at the molten heat in his eyes.

"You forgot my extra coleslaw," Lana said, inadvertently breaking the moment between them.

"Since when do you order extras of anything?" Garrett asked, seating himself beside Mimi. "You've never been a big eater."

"I've never eaten for two before."

Garrett's jaw sagged. "You mean...?"

"That's right." Lana smiled. "You're going to be an uncle again."

"Congratulations," Mimi said as Garrett gave his sister a hug. "You must be very excited."

"Dylan and I are both thrilled." Lana picked up her plastic fork. "And Greg will love having a baby brother or sister so close to his own age. Even if we will have our hands full with two kids in diapers!"

"Well, if you ever need a baby-sitter," Garrett said, his mouth curving in a half smile, "you know who to call."

"Shelby?" Lana teased.

He nodded. "That's exactly right."

They both laughed while Mimi looked back and forth between them. She envied their easy banter and the obvious love between them. She also wondered, not for the first time, how her life would have been different if she'd had a brother or a sister. Would her father have been happier with a son? Would she have always been so anxious to please him if she wasn't an only child? Would she have felt so obligated to make him happy?

"How about you, Mimi?" Lana asked, scooping up a forkful of baked beans. "Do you see children in your future?"

"I don't really know," Mimi said, turning her attention to her plate and inwardly cursing the blush warming her cheeks. She could feel Garrett's gaze on her. "I hope so. I've always wanted a big family."

"Speaking of families," Garrett said, his tone turning serious. "I know Shelby has to work late at the diner tonight, but where are Michael and Jenny?"

"Jenny came down with the flu, and Michael's waiting on her hand and foot." Lana laughed. "Which is exactly as it should be."

Garrett wiped his mouth with his napkin. "Well, when Jenny's feeling better, I want to call a family meeting."

"What about?" Lana asked.

"I think we should hire another private detective to track down LeeAnn Larrimore."

Lana nibbled her lower lip. "I don't know. I've been thinking about it and wondering if it's really worth it. I mean, I want to find our birth mother as much as you do, but all we've found so far is dead ends. No matter what happens, I'll still think of Sheila Lord as our real mother. She's the one who raised and loved us."

As Mimi listened, her opinion of Lana Van Zandt rose another notch. It took more than a pregnancy to become a parent. It took maturity and responsibility. It took true courage to raise a child.

And even more courage to give one up.

"This isn't a competition about who is the best mother," he explained, setting his jaw. "It's about finding some answers. Finding the truth."

"Maybe." Lana set down her fork. "But it's obvious our birth mother doesn't want to be found. Maybe we should respect her wishes."

"If she didn't want to be found, she shouldn't have sent that teddy bear and those baby sweaters twenty-five years too late."

Mimi listened to them argue back and forth, hearing the empathy in Lana's voice and watching Garrett grow more and more stubborn.

"I'm not going to give up," he said at last. "Not until I find her."

"Then what?" Lana asked softly.

He hesitated. "I don't know. But I just can't let it go, Lana. Not when we've come this far."

His sister reached across the table and laid her slender, pale hand over his roughened, tanned one. "I just want you to be happy."

"I'll be happy when you bring that son of yours out to the ranch," he replied, effectively changing the subject. "I've got a pony just his size."

"Oh, no," Lana said, shaking her head. "Greg can't even sit up yet!"

"You're never too young to ride a horse."

Lana pushed her paper plate away and rose to her feet. "Maybe I'd better go find my husband before he gets the same crazy idea in his head and puts Greg on one of Connor's horses. Nice to meet you, Mimi."

She smiled. "Same here."

Lana walked toward the stable, turning to give her brother one last piece of advice. "I know it's been a really long time, Garrett, but don't forget to kiss your date good-night." Then she laughed and skipped into the stable.

A ruddy blush suffused his cheeks. "She always did drive me crazy."

"I like her," Mimi said, taking a bite of creamy coleslaw.

"I like her, too," Garrett grumbled, picking up a piece of uneaten barbecue from Lana's plate and transferring it to his. "But she still drives me crazy."

"Isn't that what little sisters are supposed to do?"

"I guess so." He turned to her. "Well, Mimi Banyon, how do you like your first barbecue so far?"

Banyon. She'd forgotten about that little lie. How many others had she told since she'd arrived at the ranch? She knew instinctively that Garrett valued the truth almost as much as he valued loyalty. Would he forgive and forget her deceptions, no matter how small? How inconsequential?

Maybe she could find a way to make it up to him. If she could help him locate his mother, maybe her little masquerade wouldn't matter.

"Is something wrong?" he asked, reaching over to wipe a smudge of barbecue sauce off her chin with his index finger.

"No," she whispered, suddenly hoping he heeded his sister's advice about that good-night kiss. "Everything is just right."

SEVERAL HOURS LATER, Garrett walked Mimi to the front porch, aware of how quiet she'd become since they'd left the barbecue. The crunch of their boots on the gravel sounded louder than usual. Ever since Lana had given him that unwelcome advice about kissing Mimi good-night, he'd been unable to think about anything else.

Hell, he was twenty-eight years old and nervous as an adolescent about kissing his date good-night. Of course, he had good reason. He'd kissed Mimi once before and knew firsthand how hard it was to *stop* kissing her.

Mimi stepped onto the front porch, then circled one of the wooden posts to look at the sky. "So many stars. You never see this many in the city."

"Do you miss it?"

She shook her head. "Not at all. I thought I might, at first. But it's so different here. It makes me feel like a different person."

He took a step closer to her. "I like you just the way you are."

She looked at him. "Really?"

He was surprised at the doubt he heard in her voice. How could a beautiful woman like Mimi Banyon ever question her own appeal? He reached out one hand and gently traced the curve of her cheek. "Really."

She placed one hand on his chest, her tentative touch sucking the breath from his throat. "I happen to like you, too, Garrett Lord."

One corner of his mouth tipped up in a smile. "You don't think I'm too bossy?"

"Nothing I can't handle."

He took a step closer to her. "Are you sure?"

"Depends." Her voice was softer, almost a whisper. "What exactly do you want me to do?"

"Guess."

She licked her lips, her gaze never leaving his face. "Put the pickup away?"

"Nope."

"Check the cows?"

"Nope."

"Tuck Hubert in for the night?"

''Not even close.'' He closed the distance between them, until he could feel her soft breasts skimming his shirtfront. ''I want you to kiss me, Mimi.''

She swallowed hard. ''I thought you'd never ask.'' Then she wound her slender arms around his neck and lifted her lips to his, finally quenching the thirst that had plagued him all evening.

Garrett wrapped his arms tightly around her waist, then he lifted her off the ground to give him better access to her mouth. Sometime during that long, deep kiss, he set her on the porch rail, her legs falling open just far enough for him to step between them.

His heart pounded hard in his chest as Mimi's kiss went on and on and on. She teased him with her tongue, fanning the delicious flames inside him.

''You're so beautiful,'' he said, dropping tiny kisses on her jaw and nose and cheeks. ''So damn beautiful. Kiss me again.''

She followed his orders without a murmur of protest. He groaned low in his chest as she pulled him closer. Close enough to smell the elusive apple scent of her hair. Close enough to hear her small gasp when his hands slid from her waist to her breasts, his thumbs lightly brushing the tips.

''Tell me when to stop,'' he said huskily.

''Never,'' she whispered, then kissed him again. Her fingers found the buttons of his shirt, smoothly gliding them free.

He closed his eyes as the last one fell open, the cool night breeze caressing his bare chest, soon followed by the even gentler touch of her fingers. Her slender hands slid up his chest and over his shoulders, peeling off his shirt and dropping it onto the porch floor.

"That's much better," she whispered against his mouth.

His fingers shook as he found the small pearl buttons on her silk blouse, clumsily undoing each one. He leaned down to place a kiss on her collarbone, glimpsing the delicate white lace of her bra.

"Garrett," she breathed, tilting her head back.

His lips gently traced the valley between her breasts, his tongue skimming the lacy edge of her bra. Her hands dipped inside the waistband of his jeans, prickling his skin and sending his pulse into orbit. Blood roared in his ears as he lifted his head.

Mimi's cheeks were flushed, and her blue eyes shone bright in the moonlight. "What now, cowboy?"

He took one deep breath, then two, hoping it would help some blood return to his brain. He knew she was vulnerable. Knew she'd been ready to marry another man just a week ago. But despite his good intentions, he couldn't stop touching her. His mouth found hers again, and all his doubts melted in the heat that sizzled between them.

Their touches grew more urgent, and when her hands slid into the back pockets of his jeans and pressed him tightly against her, Garrett moaned into her mouth.

Without breaking the kiss, he scooped her up in his arms and carried her inside the house.

Hubert barked once as they crossed the threshold,

then watched in silence as Garrett carried her toward the bedroom.

This time he didn't intend to leave.

CHAPTER NINE

MIMI DIDN'T let herself think about anything except losing herself in Garrett's kiss. They stood in his bedroom, lit by the lamp on his bed stand and the moonlight streaming in through the window. She smoothed her hands over his hard chest, aware of the fast beat of his heart. Her heart raced in anticipation as he slowly backed her toward the bed, his mouth feathering light kisses across her lips and his hands fumbling with the clasp of her lacy white bra.

It fell away, and she heard the intake of Garrett's breath as he lowered his eyes to her bare breasts. The shadows in the room couldn't conceal the heat in his gaze.

"This is crazy," he breathed at the same moment his hand reached out to cup her breast.

"Insane," she murmured, closing her eyes at the myriad sensations rolling through her. Desire. Heat. Longing. No man had ever made her feel like this.

"You're delicious," he murmured, his mouth nuzzling the tender skin beneath her ear.

Her hands rested on his broad shoulders, her fingers flexing against his taut muscles.

He tenderly kissed her lips again, his knuckles brushing her cheeks. Then he drew back and looked at her. "You are so damn beautiful."

She stood on her toes to press a kiss on his chin, then laid her cheek on his chest. It grazed against soft russet hair and a taut nipple. He sucked in his breath as she turned to circle her tongue over it. Then her gaze fell on his scar, and she reached up to trace the puckered edges with her fingertips.

"Oh, Garrett," she murmured, realizing how close that bullet had come to piercing his heart. How close she'd come to losing him before she'd even met him.

"We all have scars," he whispered, catching her fingers in his hand and drawing her closer for another kiss. "Some are on the outside and some are on the inside."

Then he kissed her long and deep, and she forgot about everything except how much she wanted him to touch her again. She moaned low in her throat as his hands slid along her bare skin, over her ribs and down to her waist. His fingers worked the button on the waistband of her jeans.

We all have scars.

Mimi stiffened and stepped away from him. There was just enough light in the room for her to see his brow furrow.

"What's wrong?"

"I…" Her voice trailed off as she struggled to find a reasonable explanation for her sudden reticence. *We all have scars.* She did, too. One he would certainly see if he removed her jeans. One he would ask her about. Or, more likely, figure out for himself.

She closed her eyes, wishing she could tell him the truth. But she'd never told anyone before. And she had good reason to believe Garrett wouldn't understand.

"I'm sorry," she said at last, knowing how inadequate it sounded. At best, he'd accuse her of being a tease. At worst, he'd demand she leave.

But he didn't do either one. Instead, he walked to the window and braced his palms against the walnut frame. Then he pressed his forehead against the cool glass, breathing deeply.

She grabbed the terry-cloth robe off the end of the bed and hastily put it on. White-hot desire still pulsed inside her, and she wasn't sure she could resist if Garrett pulled her into his arms again.

But he didn't try to touch her. Instead, he turned to her, regret etched into his face. "I'm the one who's sorry, Mimi. Hell, I knew you weren't ready for this."

"It's not your fault," she assured him, feeling more guilty with each passing moment. This definitely wasn't the way she wanted their magical evening to end.

He took a step toward her. "Mimi…"

"You can sleep in your own bed tonight," she said, backing toward the door. "It's my turn to take the sofa."

"That's not necessary," he began, coming another step closer.

"I insist." With a force of will she didn't know she possessed, she looked into his eyes. "Thank you for a lovely evening, Garrett."

"Mimi, wait."

But she'd already whirled for the door, and nothing could make her stop. Tears of frustration blurred her vision as she walked into the living room, her arms wrapped around her waist. She wept silently, praying Garrett wouldn't follow her.

To her relief, his bedroom door stayed closed. She sank down on the sofa, trying to ignore Hubert, who danced around her ankles. At last, she reached down and picked him up, burying her hot, wet face in his fur.

"I'm such an idiot," she said as Hubert's tongue licked the tears off her cheeks.

She leaned back against the sofa with Hubert perched on her lap. "How could I let things go so far?"

Hubert cocked his head.

She ran a finger over her swollen lower lip, remembering how Garrett's passion had sparked her own. How easily she'd fallen into his arms. How very willing she'd been to fall into his bed.

"How am I ever going to face him tomorrow?" she asked Hubert as she lay on the sofa and drew the lonestar quilt over her body.

Hubert settled in next to her feet, resting his jaw on her ankle, then heaved a long sigh.

She closed her eyes, worried about an even bigger problem. *How am I ever going to be able to leave him?*

"I'M A DAMNED FOOL," Garrett said as he scooped oats into Peanut's trough. "I can't believe I tried to seduce a woman still in love with her fiancé."

It wasn't close to dawn yet, but Garrett had tossed and turned in his bed long enough. His *empty* bed. At last, he'd gotten up, dressed and made his way to the barn. At least there he wasn't tortured by the thought of Mimi sleeping only a few feet away from him.

He hadn't looked at her when he left. He'd been

afraid she might be awake. Afraid he might not be able to walk away from her this time. Hell, he'd barely survived it the first time.

He thrust one hand through his rumpled hair as he sank down on a bale of hay. A man shouldn't have to live with this kind of temptation. She'd told him she wasn't engaged any longer, but did she still have feelings for her fiancé?

She didn't kiss like a woman in love with another man. He didn't even want to think about her touching another man as she'd touched him last night. Another man looking at that breathtaking body of hers. And Garrett had only seen half of it.

Just enough to leave him wanting more.

"Garrett?"

His heart skipped a beat at the sound of her voice. He swallowed hard. "Yeah?"

Mimi stepped into the barn, her arms wrapped around her waist. "What are you doing out here?"

"Chores," he replied, wishing she didn't look so adorable. She wore a pair of blue overalls she'd purchased, along with a bright orange farm hat with furry ear flaps and a pair of cowboy boots that fit her properly.

He wrenched his gaze away from her and bent to scoop up another bucket of oats. "I wanted to get an early start. We've got a big day ahead of us."

She closed the barn door behind her, then took off the hat, her blond curls delectably tousled. "What do you want me to do?"

The question echoed between them, reminding him of a similar question last night.

What exactly do you want me to do?

Kiss me.

Mimi's cheeks burned, making it obvious her memory was just as good as his. She tucked an errant curl behind one ear. "I can make breakfast."

He cleared his throat. "That sounds good. I'm going to clean out the stalls, so I'll be there in about half an hour."

"All right." She stood for a moment, almost as if she wanted to say something more. Then, without another word, she turned on the heel of her cowboy boot and walked out the barn door.

Three weeks. Three more weeks to keep her at arm's length. It might as well be an eternity. Especially now that he knew how she felt in his arms.

He wondered if it would take her the entire three weeks to get over her fiancé.

Garrett picked up a pitchfork, not sure he wanted to know the answer. The best thing he could do now was forget last night ever happened. Treat her like any other ranch hand.

And take a hell of a lot of cold showers.

MIMI AND GARRETT developed a routine over the next week. They rose early, worked hard and avoided each other as much as possible. They definitely avoided any mention of the passionate night that had almost happened between them.

For the first few days, Mimi wondered if she'd be better off back in Austin. But she found solace in her work. Riding fence lines and caring for the cattle left her little time to feel sorry for herself. Calving season started in earnest, with three or four calves born each day. She learned to operate the calf pullers without fainting, though she used them only as a last resort.

Garrett didn't take her target shooting again. Or attempt to kiss her. But despite the fact that she tried to avoid prolonged conversations with him, it didn't stop her from watching him whenever she had the chance.

Saturday afternoon, exactly one week after the barbecue, was just such an occasion. She stood in the living room near the large bay window, parting the drapes just far enough to watch him chop wood for the fireplace. He'd removed his shirt, his skin glistening with sweat and his muscles straining as he wielded the ax.

She flexed her fingers on the drapes, remembering how those muscles had felt under her touch. She closed her eyes and took a deep breath, willing herself to think about mucking out the horse stalls. Whenever her thoughts strayed in the wrong direction, she made herself think about shoveling manure. It was one of the worst jobs on the ranch, and one she found herself doing far too often.

But at least it kept her busy.

The telephone rang, startling her from her thoughts. She turned away from the window and picked up the receiver. "Lord ranch."

"Is this Mimi?"

She smiled when she recognized Dr. Hawkins's nasal voice. "Yes, how nice to hear from you."

"Sorry it took me so long to get back to you. I had to attend a symposium in San Antonio last week. But it did give me a chance to consult with some of my colleagues about that unusual teddy bear you told me about.''

Her fingers tightened around the phone cord. "What did you find out?"

"That it's even more rare than I thought. If it's the genuine article. There's one way to find out. Lift up the tail...."

"Wait just a minute, please," she said, then set down the receiver and raced for Garrett's bedroom. The teddy bear sat untouched upon his dresser. She hesitated a moment, remembering all that had happened the last time she'd been in this room. Then she grabbed the teddy bear, thankful it couldn't talk.

She hurried into the living room and picked up the phone receiver. "Okay, go ahead."

"You should find a small emblem embroidered on the underside of the tail."

She lifted the tail of the teddy bear, tracing the faded red stitching with one finger. "It's a heart with the initials A.B. inside of it."

"That's it!" Dr. Hawkins didn't try to hide his excitement. "I believe you've got yourself a genuine Bruner Bear. That's worth quite a little bundle, Mimi."

She sat on the sofa. "The value doesn't matter to me at the moment. I need to know the history."

"It's short and sweet. Bruner Bears were handmade by a woman named Anna Bruner in Calloway, Texas, between the years 1909 and 1912."

Her pulse picked up a notch. "Did you say Calloway?"

"That's right. I thought that would get your attention."

Calloway, Texas, was in Sagebrush County, home

of the Sagebrush Conservation Society. Not only would they have information about the Bruner teddy bears and their creator, they might even have sale records. Or letters. Or something that could lead to information about LeeAnn Larrimore.

"I don't suppose you have a telephone number for the director of the Sagebrush Conservation Society?"

"As a matter of fact I do."

Mimi picked up a pencil and jotted down the number Dr. Hawkins recited. Then she hugged the teddy bear to her chest. "Dr. Hawkins, I don't know how I'll ever thank you."

"Just let me take a look at the Bruner Bear sometime. It's not every day you find a treasure like that."

Mimi hung up the phone, realizing Dr. Hawkins had no idea about the potential of this teddy bear. It was the key not only to the past, but possibly to the future. If it could lead to Garrett's mother, would he finally be able to put his bitterness and unanswered questions to rest?

She turned toward the door, anxious to tell Garrett the good news. Then she hesitated. What if it was just another false lead? What if it got his hopes up for nothing?

Realizing the last thing she wanted to do was disappoint him, Mimi turned to the telephone and picked up the receiver.

Then she placed a call that could change his life forever.

PAUL RENQUIST walked into the restaurant, pleased to see Harper already waiting for him. It was time for the man to start earning his inflated fee.

"Why the urgent meeting?" Harper asked as Paul sat across from him. "I was planning to come to your office tomorrow morning and give you an update. Not that I have much to report."

"This couldn't wait." Paul waved to the waitress. Then he dropped his bombshell. "I received a visit from the police today."

Harper's eyes widened. "Did Rupert bring them in on the case?"

Paul shook his head. "No, they're not even aware Mimi is missing. In fact, they came to the house looking for her. Seems they just recovered her stolen car."

"Stolen?"

"That's right. The cops raided a local chop shop and found Mimi's convertible among the cars. It had been stripped and repainted, but it still had the vehicle identification number etched on the motor. That's how they traced it to her."

Harper sat up. "This is good."

"It gets even better. The small-time punk they collared is playing the cooperation game in hopes of reducing his sentence. According to the cops, he's more than willing to answer any and all questions."

"So you want me to pay him a visit?"

"I think that would be an excellent idea. The police mentioned he was out on bond. But they gave me his name. Gordon Snyder."

Harper jotted in his notepad, then flipped it shut. "I hope Mr. Snyder can tell me exactly where he came upon Mimi's car. For his sake."

"We're close, Harper. Very close. I can feel it."

"Close enough to let Rupert in on the news?"

"Not yet." Paul steepled his fingers. "I'll wait until we actually locate his daughter. Then he can't blame me if this lead doesn't pan out."

Harper stared at him. "Are you concerned at all about your fiancée? Despite that postcard, she could possibly be the victim of a kidnapping."

"There's been no ransom note," Paul said, dismissing the idea with a flick of his hand. "And no sign of foul play. No, I think Mimi's just holed up somewhere."

"You're probably right," Harper said with a shrug. "But what if she doesn't want to be found?"

"Then I'll just have to find a way to flush her out."

GARRETT LOOKED OUT the kitchen window into the dark night as thunder rumbled in the distance. A flash of lightning illuminated the path to the barn, but he didn't see any sign of Mimi.

"Where the hell is she?" he muttered as another crack of lightning made the kitchen light flicker. He couldn't remember when it had rained so much. It was an unusual calving season—in more ways than one.

He glanced at his watch and muttered an oath under his breath. He and Mimi had been taking turns checking the cattle at night, and she'd already been gone for almost two hours. Looking out the window once again, Garrett debated whether he should go out there and find her.

The only thing stopping him was Mimi herself. She was so damn proud of herself for handling the duties of a ranch hand. Checking up on her would only convince her he didn't trust her to do the job.

He peered into the darkness, perturbed to see that lightning had shorted out the mercury light near the barn. It was pitch black out there, except for the occasional flashes of lightning. He checked his watch again. If she wasn't back in ten minutes, he was going after her.

Nine and a half minutes later, the back door finally opened. Mimi walked inside, stomping the rainwater off her boots. It sluiced off her yellow slicker and made small puddles on the vinyl floor of the mud porch.

"I've got a small problem here," she called. "Can you give me a hand?"

Garrett hurried to the mud porch, hoping she hadn't met up with another scorpion. "What's wrong?"

"Help me take my slicker off and I'll show you what I found."

He pulled the wet slicker over her head, then stared at the tiny newborn calf cradled in her arms. "Where did he come from?"

"That dappled heifer finally had her baby." She moved past him into the kitchen. "And the poor thing is soaked to the skin. It looked half-dead by the time I found it."

He watched her lay it on the rag rug in front of the sink. "Why didn't you take him to the barn?"

"I did, at first," she said, brushing the wet tendrils of hair off her forehead. "But after I unsaddled Pooh I got an idea."

"What kind of idea?"

"You'll see," she replied, and rushed out of the kitchen. Before long she was back, armed with his hair dryer.

Garrett folded his arms across his chest. "Do you really think that's going to work?"

"I don't know why not." She plugged the dryer in the outlet, then flipped the switch. The small calf didn't move at the sudden noise or at the burst of hot air against its hide. It lay completely still, its brown head stretched out on the rug and its eyes closed.

Garrett knelt beside Mimi. "Sometimes, no matter how hard we try, they don't make it."

"This one is going to make it," she said over the blast of the blow dryer.

He watched her ruffle her fingers through the calf's wet pelt, impressed by her determination. Despite his best efforts, he lost a small number of calves every season. It only took a glance at this one to see it was a goner.

But thirty minutes later, Garrett wasn't so sure of his prognosis. The calf opened its big brown eyes and blinked at him, although it still hadn't lifted its head.

"Should we call a vet?" Mimi asked, worrying her lower lip with her teeth.

"Let's try something first." Garrett moved to the cupboard and pulled out an oversize baby bottle. He filled half of it with warm water, then added a glucose solution he kept for bovine emergencies.

The calf balked at the bottle at first, but Garrett pried its mouth open and stuck the rubber nipple inside. Mimi held the calf's head on her lap, gently running her hand over its dry pelt and crooning encouraging words in its ear.

At last the calf began to suck. Awkwardly at first, then with increasing gusto.

Mimi grinned at Garrett. "I think he's going to make it!"

He nodded. "I think you're right."

After the calf had emptied the bottle, she bent and planted a kiss on top of its fuzzy head. It let out a loud, plaintive cry.

"He wants his mama," Mimi said as the calf struggled to stand up.

Garrett reached out and pulled the gangly calf into his arms. "I'll take him out to the barn and bed him down in some fresh straw. Then I'll bring his mama in and pen her up with him."

Mimi rose slowly to her feet. "Will she accept him now that he's been gone so long?" Despite her short apprenticeship as a ranch hand, she'd already learned that separating a newborn calf from its mother could result in the cow not recognizing the scent of her own offspring and thus rejecting it.

"If she doesn't, we're going to be washing a lot of baby bottles." He set the calf down briefly in the mud porch while he donned a slicker and his cowboy hat. "Don't worry, I won't leave him alone with her until I know for sure. And don't wait up for me, either. It may take all night."

A flash of lightning greeted him as he opened the back door. He picked the calf up in his arms, covering most of it with his slicker, then headed outside. The calf looked mournfully at him as raindrops pelted them both.

"Don't look at me like that," Garrett muttered. "You're the one she kissed."

Hubert barked at his heels as Garrett raced toward the barn, slipping and sliding on the muddy path. But he managed to get them both inside while they were still fairly dry.

He flipped on the overhead light, then prepared a stall as the calf attempted his first wobbly steps. It took Garrett another twenty minutes to locate the calf's mother and herd her inside the barn. By this time both he and his horse were thoroughly soaked. He unsaddled Brutus, then gave him an extra measure of oats for his trouble.

He'd just emptied the bucket into the trough when lightning flashed again, and the overhead light went out. He swore softly under his breath, then looked out the barn window toward the house. No lights burned in the windows, which meant the entire ranch had lost electricity.

Feeling his way through the darkness, Garrett finally reached the tack room. He kept a battery-operated lantern hanging by the door for just such an emergency. Storms were few and far between in the hill country, but they could be ferocious.

"Want some company?"

Garrett turned, and the glow of the lantern illuminated Mimi standing just inside the barn door. She held a big yellow bowl in her hands and had his battered thermos tucked under one arm.

"What are you doing here?" he asked.

"I thought we should celebrate Sunbeam's survival."

"Sunbeam?" he echoed, unable to stop the smile that rose to his lips. "What kind of name is that for a calf? And a bull calf, at that."

"It's the brand name of the blow dryer." She

grinned at him. "I thought we should give the manufacturer a little of the credit."

Mimi set down the bowl and thermos, then walked to the new calf's pen. Garrett joined her there, and they silently watched the mama cow sniff suspiciously at the calf. Sunbeam wobbled on his four spindly legs, but he didn't fall down.

"She's not convinced it's her calf," Garrett said softly. "The combination of the rain, blow dryer and our hands gave him a scent that's unfamiliar to her."

"Has he tried to milk yet?"

He shook his head. "She won't let him."

Mimi looked at him, a worried frown creasing her brow. "What should we do?"

"Wait." He nodded toward the cow. "She's still trying to make up her mind." Then he looked at the bowl. "Do I smell popcorn?"

"That's right. I've got hot chocolate, too. If you can find us a clean blanket, we'll be all set for a midnight picnic."

Garrett grabbed a couple of old saddle blankets out of the tack room, then laid them out in the center aisle. Mimi knelt on one blanket, then handed the thermos to Garrett. "I can't get this open."

He applied a little pressure until the lid loosened, then inhaled the comforting aroma of hot chocolate. "Did you bring some cups?"

"No, we'll have to share." She pried the lid off the bowl of popcorn. "I'm just lucky I got this made before the electricity went out."

He sat beside her. "I've never been to a midnight picnic before. What exactly are we supposed to do?"

"Have fun." She held the bowl out to him, and he

scooped up a handful of popcorn. "My mother let me have a midnight picnic for my twelfth birthday. She even stayed up with me, since my father was still at the office."

Garrett munched contentedly on his buttery popcorn, unable to take his gaze from her face. She had the most beautiful eyes he'd ever seen. "Sounds like he was a workaholic."

Mimi munched quietly for a moment. "It only got worse after my mother died when I was fourteen."

"That must have been rough."

When she finally spoke, he could hear the heartache in her words. "I still miss her."

He wanted to hold her in his arms. Instead, he reached for the thermos. "We better drink this before it gets cold."

"Good idea," she said, holding out the plastic thermos lid.

"You don't talk much about your family," he said as he carefully poured hot chocolate into the cup. Then he recapped the thermos.

Mimi leaned back against a wooden post and blew gently on the steaming chocolate. "Neither do you."

"I've told you about my adopted parents and my sisters and Michael. You've already met Lana."

"But you haven't told me why you're so determined to find your birth mother."

He scooped up another handful of popcorn, suddenly wishing he'd never brought up the subject of family. "She owes us some answers."

"Owes you? Wasn't it enough that she made certain you found a good home?"

"No." His reply was sharper than he intended. He

took a deep breath and tried to put his tangled feelings into words. "She dumped us on a doorstep with nothing more than a note and name tags. The least she could have done was stick around long enough to make certain someone found us."

Mimi took a sip of the hot chocolate, then handed the cup to him. "How do you know she didn't?"

"What?"

"How do you know she didn't watch over all of you from a distance until she was certain you were in Megan Maitland's safekeeping?"

He took a quick gulp of the hot chocolate, scalding his tongue. "There's no reason to believe she did."

"And no reason to believe she didn't."

He looked at Mimi. "Why are you so eager to defend her?"

"I'm not. I just..." She let her words trail off with a small shrug. "This is no way to conduct a party. And it's certainly not what I had in mind for our picnic."

Garrett was more than happy to change the subject. He leaned back against a straw bale, listening to the rain patter on the barn roof and enjoying the way the lamplight silhouetted Mimi's luscious body. "So what exactly did you have in mind?"

She smiled. "How about a little romance?"

His pulse picked up a notch. "Now you've got my attention."

"Good." She pulled a familiar red leather book from underneath her slicker. "Because we're about to read the continuing saga of Katherine MacGuire."

He groaned, more than a little disappointed. "Not more love behind the hog shed."

She scooted closer to him, adjusting the lantern so

that the light spilled onto the open pages of the journal. "Just listen."

January 15, 1899
Boyd proposed to me! We met behind the hog shed after supper. He gave me a whole passel of beautiful wildflowers, then went down on one knee. I told him I'd be honored to be his wife. I cried a little, too, but then sunflowers have always given me the sniffles.

Boyd wants to start up a ranch of his own near San Antonio. He's got people there who will help him. He talked half the night about his dreams for the ranch and the wonderful house he'll build for us.

Oh, if only Pa will give us his blessing! Boyd said he isn't afraid to face him, but all the rest of the ranch hands almost jump out of their britches when Pa starts yelling at them.

Just think, in a few days I'll be a bride. We're lucky the circuit preacher is in the area. Now I just need to find something old, something new, something borrowed and something blue.

I'll wear my new yellow dress for the wedding. And borrow a yellow hair ribbon from Minnie Jo to wear in my hair. That takes care of something new and something borrowed. And I know Ma will be plenty blue when she hears the news. That just leaves something old.

Maybe Boyd can help me think of something.

January 16, 1899
He's gone. I looked everywhere for Boyd after

breakfast this morning and couldn't find him.
Then Hank told me he snuck off in the middle
of the night. And stole one of Pa's horses! I don't
believe it. I know it can't be true. Boyd loves
me. He asked me to marry him. Something terrible must have happened to make him leave.

No matter what Ma says, I know he'll come
back for me. I just know it.

Mimi looked up from the journal. "Looks like
things are definitely getting worse for our star-crossed
lovers."

Garrett could sympathize with the young couple.
Things were definitely getting worse for him, too.

He was falling in love with his ranch hand.

Heat crawled over his skin at the revelation. How
could he fall in love with a woman he'd just met two
weeks ago? A woman he suspected was still in love
with another man. It was preposterous. Insane.

And an undeniable fact. He loved her. Now he just
had to figure out what to do about it.

She began reading again, and he closed his eyes,
savoring the sound of her voice.

February 1, 1899
No word from Boyd. Every day I watch the horizon for him, but every night I go to bed with a
broken heart. I can't wait any longer. Tonight I
will follow after the man I love. If I head south
for San Antonio, I may meet up with people who
have seen Boyd. Maybe he's gone on ahead to
buy our ranch.

I'll leave a note for Ma and I'll leave my dear journal in my special hiding place in the barn. Someday I'll come back and record my journey.

I just know it will end happily ever after.

Garrett opened his eyes to see Mimi closing the journal.

"Well, don't leave me in suspense," he teased. "What happened?"

She looked at him, a frown creasing her brow. "I don't know. That's the last entry."

"Are you sure?"

She sat up straighter and quickly thumbed through the slim journal again. "Positive. All the rest of the pages are blank."

"So Katherine took off after Boyd...."

"And she never came back."

[faint text visible from reverse side of page]

CHAPTER TEN

"I FOUND HER."

Paul shot to his feet, as surprised to see Harper standing in the library of the Casville mansion as he was to hear the news. "Keep your voice down!"

He strode to the door, taking a look around the empty hallway before closing it and turning the lock. His heart beat triple time in his chest. Sleepless nights and tension-filled days placating Mimi's distraught father had taken their toll. Rupert had even started making noises about going to the police and declaring his daughter a missing person, which meant all of Paul's well-laid plans were about to unravel.

"Where is she?" he asked, wiping his damp palms on the front of his slacks.

Harper waited until he sat down behind the desk. "Five miles east of Austin as the crow flies. A place called the Lord ranch."

Paul frowned. "What is that? Some kind of dude ranch for the rich and famous?"

"No. It's a working ranch. Owned by one Garrett Lord."

"So how did you find out she was there?"

"After I talked with Snyder, I started canvassing the rural area where he claimed he found her abandoned car. I got lucky my first time out at a ranch called the Triple C. The owner didn't know anything, but his daughter, Venna Schwab, recognized Mimi's picture right away." Harper smiled. "That Venna is quite a number."

"I don't give a damn about some cowgirl. Tell me about Mimi. What's she doing at a ranch?"

"Working."

Paul snorted. "Good one, Harper. Let's save the jokes until after we've got this deal sewn up."

"I'm not joking. She's apparently hired on as a ranch hand."

Paul shook his head. "Mimi's never done a day of hard labor in her life. She spends her time cataloguing musty antiques and filling out the branches of the great and powerful Casville family tree. There has to be some other explanation."

"Well, it's probably not going to be one you like." Harper took a seat on the sofa. "Venna claims Mimi is living with Garrett Lord. They even attended a neighborhood barbecue together a couple of weeks ago. Perhaps there's more to their relationship than business."

Paul clenched his jaw, surprised at his reaction. Jealousy wasn't his style. But it galled him that Mimi was shacking up with another man so soon after their botched nuptials. Any remnants of guilt he had left about relieving her father of a few million dollars mercifully disappeared.

"So what now?" Harper asked.

Paul pressed the tips of his fingers together. Knowing Mimi's precise location changed everything. He'd have to proceed very carefully. "Let me think about it. In the meantime, keep her under surveillance."

"And if she heads for home?" Harper asked.

Paul leveled his gaze on him. "Then make sure she doesn't get there."

THE NEXT DAY, Garrett stood on the edge of the hayloft and pitched another forkful of straw into the stall below. Unfortunately, the work didn't distract him from thinking about Mimi. She'd left in his pickup this morning on some mysterious errand. He couldn't help but wonder if she'd gone to meet with her fiancé.

He stabbed the fork into the straw, telling himself it didn't matter. Calving season was almost over. Then Mimi would be gone for good.

Unless he could think of a damn good reason for her to stay.

"Garrett?"

"Up here," he called, shaking the packed straw loose from the pitchfork.

A few moments later, Mimi appeared at the top of the ladder. She sneezed at the dust in the air, then smiled as she walked toward him. "I have a surprise for you."

He stuck the pitchfork into a square bale of straw. "Now, that sounds intriguing."

"Here it is." She held up a bulky manila envelope.

He took a step closer to her.

"What is it?"

"Your past."

Garrett looked up from the envelope into her sparkling blue eyes. "I don't understand."

She took a deep breath. "When I saw your teddy bear, I knew it was special. So I called a friend of mine, a professor who specializes in antique toys. After I gave him a detailed description, he confirmed that the teddy bear is very unique. A limited number were made and sold over ninety years ago in the Sagebrush County area."

He stared at the envelope. "Why didn't you tell me?"

"Because I didn't want you to be disappointed if it was another dead end." She pushed the package into his hands. "But it's not, Garrett."

He sank down on a bale of straw, then fumbled with the clasp of the envelope, surprised to find his fingers shaking. "Damn."

"Let me do it." She leaned over his shoulder, her blond hair caressing his cheek.

He closed his eyes, trying to regain his equilibrium. After searching for answers for so long, they were now quite literally in his grasp. He should be ecstatic. Instead, his curiosity had turned to wariness. What if there was something inside that envelope he didn't want to know? What if it was something that could change his life forever?

"Garrett? Are you all right?"

He opened his eyes and saw Mimi seated beside him. She held a thick blue book in her hands with the title *Calloway Centennial 1885-1985* emblazoned in silver lettering across the front.

He cleared his throat. "Of course."

She scooted closer and began slowly paging through the book. "This is a compilation of the history of Calloway, Texas, a tiny town north of San Antonio. There are old photographs in here, as well as information about the first settlers in the area."

He could hear the underlying excitement in her

voice. Her fascination with the past was obvious, and he could see she'd chosen her career well. Which made him wonder all over again why she would put her life on hold just to work on a cattle ranch.

Mimi turned to the middle of the book and pointed to a photocopy of a daguerreotype. In it was an older couple, the man looking fierce with his long white beard, the woman short and plump with big dark eyes. "This is Samuel Larrimore. Your great-great-grandfather."

Garrett swallowed hard as he stared at the photo, looking for some resemblance. "And that's my great-great-grandmother beside him?"

She nodded. "Helga Bruner Larrimore. She was Samuel's third cousin, a widow who lived in Germany. When Samuel was forty-five years old, he wrote to her and asked her to marry him. She accepted, and came to Calloway in 1885 with her three-year-old daughter, Anna Bruner, in tow."

Garrett looked up from the book. "How do you know all this?"

Mimi smiled. "I contacted the director of the Sagebrush Conservation Society several days ago. A very helpful lady. When I learned she was going to be in Austin today for a symposium, I asked her to meet me and bring any materials she'd discovered related to Larrimores. Including photocopies of old letters, birth certificates, marriage licenses and death notices. This centennial book was an unexpected bonus."

Relief flowed through him. "So that was the reason for your mysterious errand."

She nodded. "I had to take your teddy bear with me, too. The director made me promise to let her look at an authentic Bruner Bear. But don't worry. It's back safe and sound in your bedroom.''

"A Bruner Bear?''

"Designed and crafted by Anna Bruner. Your great-aunt.''

He shook his head. "I still can't believe you learned all this from one worn-out old teddy bear.''

"Garrett, that worn-out old teddy bear is worth over a thousand dollars.''

He blinked. "What?''

"It's true,'' she said, laughing at his stunned expression. "Teddy bears became popular around 1906, and Anna Bruner began making her bears in 1909. She died in 1912, when she was only thirty years old. So Bruner bears are not only of exceptional quality, but very rare. You own one of the few left in existence.''

He turned to the book. "Are there any other Larrimores in here?''

She flipped the page and pointed to a photograph of a family of eight. Five young girls in identical frilly dresses and one young boy wearing a dark, homespun suit all stood staring stiffly at the camera. Their mother sat proudly among her children, three on either side of her. She was a petite woman with a sprinkling of freckles and a mischievous gleam in her eyes that reminded Garrett a little bit of Lana.

Mimi pointed to the father in the picture, a man with short dark hair parted straight down the middle and a handlebar mustache. "That's Wilhelm Larrimore. He's the only son of Samuel and Helga.''

"These are my great-grandparents,'' Garrett said, staring at the photo.

"That's right. And the boy in the picture is your grandfather, Hans Larrimore."

Garrett brushed his finger over the photo, his throat tight. To be finally given a past, a heritage of his very own, after all these years was almost too much for him to comprehend.

"Hans married a woman named Stella, and they had one child in 1942. A son."

"My father?" Garrett ventured, his voice so tight it came out in a whisper.

"Yes." Mimi sorted through the papers in the envelope, then handed one to him. "This is his birth certificate."

Garrett took a deep breath, then read the neatly typed certificate. "'Gary Hans Larrimore. Born December 2, 1942. Mother, Stella Rimmer Larrimore. Father, Hans Larrimore.'"

He stared at the birth certificate, unable to believe it was real. "My father's name is Gary Larrimore."

Mimi laid her hand over his. He grasped it, hanging on tight as his well-ordered world tilted on its axis. After twenty-five years, he finally knew his father's name.

"There's more." Mimi handed him another piece of paper. "This is your grandfather's obituary. He was drafted into the Army during World War Two, shortly after your father's birth." Her voice softened. "He never made it home."

"'Sergeant Hans Larrimore, 27, of rural Sagebrush County,'" Garrett read aloud, noting the date, 1943, at the top of the obituary, "'was killed in action somewhere in the Pacific theater. Hans leaves behind his loving wife, Stella, and son, Gary. Also mourning his death are his parents, Wil and Kate Larrimore, and his grandmother, Mrs. Helga Larrimore. Memorial services will be held Friday at the Calvary Lutheran Church in Calloway.'''

Blood pounded in his ears. It was too much. After almost three decades of seeing nothing but a big black hole in his past, it was rapidly filling with family and faces. Joys and sorrows. He let the obituary fall out of his fingers and flutter to his lap. "What else do we know?"

Mimi still held his hand and gave it a gentle, encouraging squeeze. Then she opened the centennial book. "There's a section in here on each of the families who settled in Calloway and the surrounding area. The Larrimores were one of those families."

"And?" he prompted, almost afraid to get his hopes up.

"And it lists all their descendants up to the present day. I haven't had a chance to look through everything yet. But I did find this."

She cleared her throat and began reading in the middle of the Larrimore family history. "'"After the death of Hans Larrimore, his wife, Stella, left the area with her young son, Gary. Many years later, word was received that Stella had passed away and that Gary had married LeeAnn Bonham of Pipecreek, Texas. We have no information if any children resulted from this union.'''

Garrett stood up and began pacing across the straw-covered loft. "They're wrong. There are children. Me. Michael. Shelby. Lana."

"You're not upset, are you?"

"Upset?" He bent and scooped Mimi off the floor.

Then he swung her around with a whoop of delight. "I can't believe it. You found them! You found my family. We're Larrimores. Children of Gary and LeeAnn Larrimore. Grandchildren of Hans Larrimore. Great-grandchildren of Wilhelm Larrimore."

She laughed when he finally set her down on the loft floor. "Don't forgot Samuel and Helga."

"And Anna," he added, his smile widening to a grin. "The woman who created the Bruner Bear."

"The key to your past," she said softly.

"You found more than the key to my past, Mimi." He took a step closer to her, his voice low and husky. "You found the key to my heart."

MIMI CLOSED HER EYES as Garrett kissed her. A deep, soul-wrenching kiss that lasted forever and bonded her to him completely. His lips skimmed over her brow and cheeks until they found her mouth once again.

She sank into him, savoring his warmth and his strength. She could feel the rock-steady beat of his heart beneath her fingertips.

"Mimi," he said softly.

When she looked up, he kissed her again. A gentle, seeking kiss that made her heart ache.

"You really know how to thank a girl," she said, trying to keep the mood light. Trying to stay strong.

He pulled back, cupping her face in his hands. His green-gold eyes were steady and somber. "This isn't gratitude, Mimi. Don't you know how many nights I've lain awake wanting you? How many days it has taken all my willpower to walk away when all I wanted to do was kiss you until you couldn't think straight?''

"Me, too," she admitted. "I just…" Her voice trailed off as she looked at him, desire and uncertainty warring within her. "I wasn't sure what you'd think of me. There are still so many things we don't know about each other, Garrett. So many things you don't know about me—"

"I know that I want you," he interjected, his voice husky in her ear.

She licked her lips, unable to resist any longer. "And I want you."

He stepped back and gave her that crooked half-smile that she loved so much. "Then we've both been idiots. Finding stupid excuses to walk away from what we both want. What we both need."

"Sometimes it's better to walk away," Mimi whispered, thinking of someone she'd walked away from. Someone precious she'd never forgotten.

"Not for us. We've wasted so much time already." He reached out one hand, tracing her lips with the pad of his thumb. "My grandfather died a young man in the war. Anna Bruner died a young woman. And God only knows what happened to my parents."

She closed her eyes, the movement of his thumb making her lips tingle. Then it left her mouth, caressing her jaw and trailing over the sensitive skin of her neck.

"We can't be afraid to live anymore, Mimi," he said, moving closer so that his body was pressed firmly against her. "Or to love."

She could feel his arousal and longed to touch him. Stroke him. Assuage this need that was consuming them both. *She wanted him so much.* But did she dare let him love her? Ripples of apprehension prickled goose bumps over her skin.

"Katherine gave up everything for love," she whispered, terrified of losing her heart. "And she never came back."

"Do you think she was sorry?" His hands moved to her shoulders, his thumbs circling just above her breasts. Her nipples grew taut, and she yearned to rise on her toes to give him better access.

"No," she said at last, her defenses crumbling under his erotic touch. Maybe the time had come for Garrett to see all her scars, inside and out. She wrapped her arms around his neck and drew him down toward her mouth. "No."

He moaned under the hot intensity of her kiss, his tongue meeting hers, circling and thrusting. Mimi reveled in the silky smoothness of his mouth as she buried her fingers in his hair.

Garrett's hand slid from her shoulders to the front of her blouse, teasing her breasts as he ever so slowly popped the buttons open one by one. He slid the blouse over her shoulders, then turned his attention to her bra. It slipped off into the straw, leaving her half-naked before him.

"Oh, Mimi," he said in wonder, reaching out for her. The touch of his rough fingertips against her bare skin made her tremble. Then he lowered his head to kiss the erect pink tip of her left breast.

Before she could speak or move, he knelt in front of her. His tongue lightly circled her nipple while his long fingers stroked her other breast. He sucked gently, his pleasure evident in the hungry growl she heard deep in his throat. She tipped back her head, wondering how much more pleasure she could take. Then he repeated his ministrations on her other breast, tasting and suckling. Arousing her almost beyond endurance while she was still half-dressed.

At last, he pulled her down into the straw until she was kneeling with him. The setting sun cast long shadows over the hayloft and illuminated the floating dust motes so they looked like golden bubbles.

He kissed her lips as he laid her on a soft bed of straw, then sat back and let his gaze wander over her until he reached her eyes. "You are so beautiful."

"Take your shirt off," she whispered, her mouth dry and her body pulsing with need.

He quickly unbuttoned his shirt, his gaze never leaving her face. The last few buttons popped off as he tugged his shirt out of his jeans and ripped it off his shoulders.

"Touch me," he pleaded, reclining on a soft bed of straw next to her.

Mimi reached out and slid her hand over the light mat of burnished hair on his chest. His skin was so incredibly warm. She ran her hand over the washboard ridges of his stomach.

He sucked in his breath as her fingers slid past his navel to his belt buckle. Mimi looked up to see his eyes closed and his jaw taut. Heady with the power she had over the strongest man she'd ever met, she leaned down to kiss the washboard ripples across his stomach while her fingers worked at undoing the buckle.

"Mimi," he breathed, his voice strained. "You don't know what you're doing to me."

"More," she whispered. "I'm doing more."

He moaned as her tongue slipped beneath the open button fly of his jeans. Then she sat up, sliding her fingers up and down the straining bulge in his blue jeans.

"No more," he gasped as she unzipped his jeans and pulled them down over his hips.

"More," she promised, straddling him to relieve the pounding need in her body.

They both moaned as his hardness met the hot core of her softness. She rubbed against him, kindling the fire between them even more. Then Garrett rolled her over, quickly shedding his jeans and boxer shorts.

Her jeans and panties followed so quickly that she barely had time to prepare herself. Naked and vulnerable, she lay before him, her body and her heart trembling with need. She held her breath as his gaze skimmed over her. Did he notice the bikini-line scar on her abdomen? Did he care?

But her apprehensions slipped away as he took her in his arms again. His warm, dewy skin kissed hers as he lay full-length upon her, their bodies seeking each other. His lips found her mouth at the same time he opened her with his fingers.

Desire clouded her mind, but she was still coherent enough to realize that they were almost to the point of no return. "Garrett," she whispered, keeping her long-ago vow never to make the same mistake twice. "I'm not on anything...birth control, I mean."

"That's all right," he whispered, reaching for his jeans and digging into the back pocket. "I'm prepared. I've been prepared ever since the night of the party. Call it wishful thinking."

He turned away from her for a moment, then he was holding her again. Kissing her. She wrapped her arms around him and held on tight, determined never to let him go.

"You're mine, Mimi," he whispered, hovering above her. "All mine."

The next moment he was inside her, and the sensation was so intensely sweet that hot tears sprang to her eyes.

Garrett kissed them away, then closed his eyes with a deep groan as he moved within her. They made love to the accompaniment of cooing barn swallows and the soft swish of a horse's tail. Mimi matched Garrett's rhythm, almost as if they heard the same wonderful music. The beat rose and fell, moving faster and faster as something molten inside of her simmered and threatened to boil over.

Garrett pressed his face against her neck, moaning deeply as his long, powerful body flexed against her. She grasped his shoulders in wonderment, then let him carry her into ecstasy. They both joined in the song, crying out in perfect harmony.

At last Mimi opened her eyes, uncertain if minutes or days had passed. Garrett lay beside her, his eyes closed and his handsome face so relaxed and content it made her heart fill with love for him.

She propped herself up on one elbow to look at him. Night had fallen, and the darkness surrounding them made her feel they were the only two people in the world.

At last Garrett opened his eyes and gave her a lazy smile. "We definitely wasted too much time."

She rippled the short russet hair on his upper thigh

with her fingertips. "Then we'd better start making up for it, cowboy."

"Good idea," he said, reaching for her once again.

PAUL SAT at the antique rosewood desk in Mimi's bedroom, methodically rifling through her drawers. Now that he'd finally located his fugitive fiancée, he'd need something to convince her to become his bride. Some kind of leverage that would insure Paul Renquist became a very wealthy man.

If he didn't hit pay dirt soon, he'd conduct a thorough search of old man Casville's study. Surely a man that rich couldn't be squeaky clean. Mimi would do anything to protect her father. Hell, she'd probably agree to marry Paul just to protect one of those snotty servants. She seemed to have a soft spot in her heart for just about everyone.

Except him.

He yanked open the last drawer and sifted through the neat stack of files. Mimi's career as an archivist had obviously made it impossible for her to throw anything away. It seemed as if he'd been up here for hours, sorting through old school papers, newspaper clippings, boring letters and other assorted Casville family junk.

He cut his finger on the open seal of an envelope as he dug into the drawer. Swearing, he yanked the drawer out and dumped the contents on the floor.

"Nothing," he muttered, smearing his blood against the scattered papers as he raked through them. He didn't know what he was looking for, but it sure as hell wasn't this worthless crap.

He picked up the drawer, haphazardly tossing the

assorted papers and files back inside. He swore again as his bloody finger scraped against the rough wood on the underside of the drawer.

Then it hit something smooth and slick. *Cellophane packaging tape.* He slowly turned the drawer over and stared at the lavender envelope taped securely to the bottom of the drawer.

''What do we have here?'' He neatly ripped the envelope from its hiding place, then opened the flap. Inside he found a letter dated August 26, 1992. Nine years ago, give or take a few months.

Dear Mimi,
I realize this letter comes as somewhat of a surprise to you. A year ago we parted ways, never expecting to see each other again. But on this special anniversary, I had to write and thank you once again. You have given us the most precious gift. B and I pray that your generosity is returned to you someday a hundredfold.

Your mistake became our blessing. Know that we treasure J every day, and will continue to do so for the rest of our lives.

Love,
D

Paul read the letter again, thoroughly perplexed. Then he looked inside the envelope once again, and his heart began pounding in his chest. He drew out a small photo of a little boy wearing a sailor suit. Big blue eyes smiled at him. Very familiar blue eyes.

Pay dirt.

CHAPTER ELEVEN

MIMI WOKE UP the next morning in Garrett's bed. Only this time she wasn't alone.

"Mornin', sleepyhead," Garrett murmured as he leaned over and pulled a piece of straw out of her hair. "I thought you'd never wake up."

She ran one finger over the stubble of whiskers on his jaw. "I suppose you want me to handle all the chores this morning so you can sleep?"

"Sounds tempting, but I'm the one who has to get up. Another customer called yesterday afternoon while you were out. He's coming here this morning to look at the bulls."

Mimi sighed, pulling the bedclothes up to her bare shoulders and wishing they could stay in bed together all day. "When?"

"Soon." Garrett kissed the tip of her nose. "Why don't you stay here and keep the bed warm? I promise I'll be back as fast as I can."

She wound her arms around his neck to keep him close to her. "Why don't you call and tell this customer to take a rain check instead? Or at least talk him into waiting until later this afternoon. Then we can both stay here and…warm up the bed."

"Don't tempt me," he murmured, then kissed her. A long, slow, deep kiss that made her forget about cattle buyers and chores and everything else a good ranch hand should have on her mind.

Garrett moaned low in his throat as her hands disappeared beneath the blankets. "On second thought…"

The loud blast of a car horn made them both groan.

"Damn," he muttered, stealing one last kiss before he climbed out of bed. "There's nothing I hate worse than an early bird."

She laughed, feeling almost giddy. "This from the man who got me out of bed before six o'clock every morning for the last three weeks."

"Well, now that I've finally got you *in* my bed," he said, reaching for his work shirt, "I'd like to keep you there for a while."

She leaned back against the pillow and watched him dress. It had been too dark to see him fully last night in the barn, but this morning sunlight streamed through the windows, allowing her to see every delectable inch of his finely honed body.

"Enjoying the view?" he asked as he buttoned his faded green work shirt.

"Definitely." She watched him step into blue boxer shorts, then pull on denim jeans. His big hands tucked the shirttails into his jeans, then zipped up the fly and buttoned the waistband.

She stretched out on his side of the mattress, the white cotton sheet still warm from his body. "Although I think I prefer watching you take your clothes off."

"I'll be happy to oblige—"

The car horn sounded again, drawing a muttered

oath from Garrett as he buckled his leather belt. "I take it this guy's in a hurry."

"Look at it this way," Mimi said, "the sooner you get out there, the sooner you can get rid of him."

"I like the way you think." He leaned down to kiss her, then nipped her earlobe. "But then, I like a lot of things about you. Your ears. Your nose. Your mouth." He kissed her again. "Definitely your mouth."

"Go," she ordered, pushing him away before they both became too distracted by the sensual electricity that pulsed between them.

He turned at the bedroom door to wink at her. "Stay warm for me." Then he was gone.

Mimi sighed, rolling to her side and pulling his pillow into her arms. It still held his scent. She closed her eyes and breathed deeply. She lay there for a few minutes, but sleep eluded her. Despite the long night of lovemaking, Mimi felt wide-awake and thoroughly refreshed.

Her stomach growled, and she looked at the clock, surprised to find it was already past ten o'clock in the morning. Throwing off the covers, she rolled out of bed, then stood naked in front of the dresser mirror.

She hardly recognized the woman staring back at her. Sparkling blue eyes and tanned, rosy cheeks. Pink lips that were just a little puffier than normal. But it was the changes on the inside that really mattered. Pure joy radiated through her.

It had finally happened.

"I'm in love," she crooned to the mirror. "I'm in love with Garrett Lord."

Her gaze fell to the faint pink scar at the base of

her abdomen. Garrett hadn't seen it last night, though she'd been ready to tell him the whole story. Part of her was thankful it hadn't come out.

And part of her wanted to tell him every little detail about her life. Every secret of her past. Every wish for her future.

Their future.

"You're getting ahead of yourself," Mimi admonished the love-struck girl in the mirror. She picked up a comb and ran it through her tangled hair. "He doesn't even know your real last name yet. And one night together does not a lifetime commitment make."

Then she sighed. "But what a night."

Another blast of the obnoxious car horn made her smile at her reflection. Her cowboy was obviously taking his sweet time. Too bad the customer didn't realize that Garrett Lord was his own man, answering to no one.

She moved toward the window and parted the curtain for a peek. The angle didn't allow her to see anything but the tail end of a silver sports car. Hubert stood by a rear tire with his leg lifted.

Then a man came into her view.

A man who could ruin everything.

GARRETT ground his teeth together as he stood on the front porch, a cup of hot coffee in his hands. The man in the flashy black cowboy suit stood with the door to his silver Jaguar open, leaning heavily on the horn.

The noise sent Hubert into a frenzy of barking. Garrett walked over to lean against the porch rail and sipped at the coffee.

At last the man caught sight of him and let up on the horn. "I'm looking for Garrett Lord."

"You found him," Garrett said, setting down his coffee cup.

The man's gaze flicked over him, and it was obvious he wasn't impressed by the faded work clothes and scuffed cowboy boots. "I'm Paul Renquist."

Living so close to Austin, Garrett was used to urban cowboys coming here and throwing their money around. This one wore cowboy clothes fresh from a designer store. Right down to his shiny new alligator-skin boots.

"I'm planning to buy a big spread," Renquist said, walking up to the porch. "And naturally, I'm only interested in premium stock."

"That's the only kind I sell."

He tipped his Stetson. "Good. Then maybe we can do business."

"What are you looking for in a bull?" Garrett kept meticulous records and could answer any questions ranging from birth weight to rate-of-gain to feed efficiency on all his breeding stock. He could also trace the genetic lines of his longhorn cattle back at least five generations. He smiled, realizing he and Mimi shared a common interest in family trees.

"Do you have any black ones?"

"Black ones?" A muscle flickered along Garrett's jaw. "Do you mean Angus?"

Renquist shrugged. "If that's what they're called."

Garrett clenched his jaw, wondering why he even bothered to get out of bed this morning. Especially when he had a beautiful woman in it. "I raise registered Texas longhorns."

The man looked clueless.

"Brown and white ones." Garrett said, bringing the conversation down to Renquist's level. Way down. "I don't have any black ones. Maybe you should try the Triple C."

To his disappointment, Renquist shook his head. "No, brown and white ones will be fine."

Garrett stepped off the porch. "Why don't I just bring my best bull into the corral. I think it will save us both time."

"Sounds good." Renquist turned to the barn, then glanced at his Jaguar. "Can you get your dog away from my car?"

Garrett bit back a smile. Hubert didn't always have the best aim. The bottom edge of the driver's door was dripping wet. "Come here, boy."

Hubert bounded over to him. Garrett reached down to rub his furry head. "Good dog," he said under his breath.

"Wait here," he told Renquist when they'd reached the corral. "I'll bring the bull out." He climbed over the fence, idly wondering why he bothered to sell some of his cattle for breeding stock. Working with the public didn't appeal to him. Hell, nothing appealed to him lately except spending time with a certain leggy blonde.

He looked up and saw her, standing on the front porch of the house. His body tightened at the sight of her. She wore blue jeans, boots and one of his old chambray shirts, the tails hanging almost to her knees. Her hair hung loose and spilled over her shoulders, gleaming gold in the morning sunlight.

It took all his willpower not to run up on the porch and kiss her senseless.

"Mr. Renquist wants to see Rowdy," Garrett called as Mimi slowly approached them.

"Rowdy?" Renquist asked, though he'd turned to stare at Mimi.

"That's the bull's name," Garrett informed him, then looked at Mimi. "Can you run the fence when I herd him into the corral?"

"Of course," she replied, her voice sounding oddly strained. She looked a little pale, too.

"Is that dangerous?" Renquist asked, turning to Garrett.

Garrett looked away from Mimi, telling himself she was probably just tired. "Don't worry, Renquist. You'll be safe if you stay outside the corral."

"I mean is it dangerous for a woman."

"This is my ranch hand," Garrett explained, motioning to her. "Mimi Banyon. Mimi, this is Paul Renquist."

Renquist doffed his cowboy hat. "A pleasure to meet you, Miss Banyon."

Garrett hesitated, tempted to tell Renquist the bull wasn't for sale. He could sense the man was more a looker than a buyer, anyway. And he didn't like the way Renquist was looking at Mimi.

"Perhaps I should run the fence," Renquist gallantly offered.

That was the last thing Garrett wanted. Either Renquist would screw up and let Rowdy out of the corral, or the feisty young bull would gore him and Garrett would have a pesky lawsuit on his hands.

"No," Mimi said abruptly, then met Garrett's gaze. "I'll do it."

He nodded, then headed for the barn, half sorry he hadn't taken Renquist up on the offer. A confrontation with Rowdy might have sent the wannabe cowboy running back to the city. Then he and Mimi could have picked up where they'd left off this morning.

With any luck, Renquist wouldn't find anything on the ranch that appealed to him and would leave empty-handed. The sooner, the better.

MIMI WAITED until Garrett was out of earshot, then she turned toward her fiancé. "What are you doing here?"

Paul leaned casually against a wooden fence post. "What do you think?"

She watched him, trying to gauge his mood. But Paul was one of the most controlled men she'd ever met. At one time, his iron control had made her feel safe. Now it scared her. "I don't know. I assume this isn't a coincidence."

He smiled. "No. I knew I'd find you here." His gaze raked over her, and his smiled widened. "I just didn't realize I'd find you looking quite so lovely."

Mimi frowned, confused by his odd behavior. She'd expected anger. Recriminations. Certainly not this easygoing, almost flirtatious demeanor. Especially since the Paul Renquist she knew could never be described as easygoing.

Something was very wrong.

"Are you ready to come home?" Paul asked at last. "Your father is lost without you. So am I."

"Stop it, Paul," she hissed. "I know my father was

paying you to marry me. I heard all about his little incentive program.'' Just the thought of it sickened her.

He shook his head. ''I don't know what you think you heard, or from whom, but it's not at all what you think. I love you, Mimi. I forgive you. And I still want to marry you.''

Her stomach lurched. ''I think you'd better leave.''

''Not without my bride.''

She took a step away from him. ''You're going to have to sell yourself to some other gullible woman, Paul. I'm not buying it anymore.''

''But you haven't even heard my price yet.''

''I won't play games with you. And I won't let you play games with Garrett.''

He sneered. ''Oh, it's Garrett, is it? Sounds like you're on pretty friendly terms with your boss. Tell me, Mimi, exactly what do your duties include?''

His cool demeanor had finally melted under the heat of his anger. It blazed in his eyes and pinched the corners of his thin mouth.

Mimi's head began to throb. She'd been fooling herself these past few weeks. Pretending she could leave her old life behind her without any repercussions.

She looked him squarely in the eye. ''That's none of your business. I know now that I was wrong to run out of the church. I should have confronted you then and there.''

''Confronted me?'' Paul moved closer to her. ''How about married me? We should be celebrating our honeymoon on a sunny Caribbean island instead of arguing in a yard full of dirt and manure.''

She suppressed a shudder at how close she'd come to throwing her life away with this man. "Maybe I should have told you the marriage was off. But then, you should have told me a few things, too. Like the fact that my father was paying for stud services."

He shook his head and gave her a patronizing smile. "You've got it all wrong, Mimi. Your father and I had simply worked out a business arrangement. He wants grandchildren, and I can happily provide them. I want money. Lots of it. And he can provide it."

Mimi stared at him, wondering how she could have been so blind to his true motives. Had she really been that lonely? That desperate for love?

At least now it was all out in the open. "Why are you really here, Paul?"

"I've been worried about you, Mimi. No one has seen or heard from you since the wedding. Except for that postcard. Your father is…a little upset."

"I'm sure that's an understatement," she said wryly.

"True. Especially after having to face down four hundred wedding guests and tell them there wasn't going to be a wedding. Then he insisted on inviting everyone to the reception, so all that food wouldn't go to waste. He left me to deal with the press, including that flaky columnist from the *American Statesman*. But I survived."

"I assumed you would."

Paul flicked a piece of lint off the sleeve of his shirt. "We told everyone you were ill. That the wedding was simply postponed."

Mimi looked at him. "But that's not true."

Paul took a step closer to her. "Surely you're not a stranger to deception, Mimi. For instance, your boss introduced you as Mimi Banyon. Is there a reason you didn't tell him your real name?"

"Fear of fortune hunters," she snapped.

He smiled. "That's not the only lie you've told, is it? After all, you've had a lot of practice. Ten years, at least."

Her heart skipped a beat. "I think you should leave."

"I will. If you come with me."

She couldn't believe his nerve. "Forget it. We're through, Paul. So you'll have to find some other way to make your fortune. Have you ever considered actually working for it?"

"Touché." Paul hitched one foot up on the fence rail. "Actually, I am looking into a career in sales."

"Planning to sell snake oil?"

He smiled. "No. Information. Very valuable information that I'm sure would appeal to your father. I just haven't decided on the right price yet."

She tipped up her chin. "I'm not afraid of my father finding out where I am."

"Maybe not. But are you afraid of your father finding out where your son is?"

She stopped breathing for a moment. "I don't know what you're talking about."

"I'm talking about little baby Joshua. Born in Paris ten years ago. Rupert's secret grandson."

Mimi sucked in a deep breath, trying to quell the panic rising within her. "You're wrong."

"Cut the crap, Mimi." Paul came one step closer to her. "It took quite a bit of digging, but I finally found the birth certificate. You were listed as the mother of Joshua Andrew.''

Raw fear welled up inside of her. "No."

"Yes." Paul moved another step closer. "We both know Rupert is obsessed with passing on his legacy. He'd stop at nothing to get his hands on Joshua. A male heir to the great Casville dynasty.''

Mimi knew it was true. Even if her father didn't have any legal right to the child, he was rich and powerful enough to make the lives of Joshua's adopted family miserable for years to come. To traumatize her son with the fear of being ripped away from the only parents he'd ever known.

She'd read about enough custody battles in the news, pitting a biological relative against an adoptive relative, to know how ugly they could get. All the lawsuits for grandparents' rights. Ultimately, it was always the children who suffered.

And what would happen when she was brought into the dispute? If she took the side of Joshua's adoptive parents, would her son believe she was rejecting him? She closed her eyes, visualizing the nightmare of a court trial. Not to mention the media circus that was sure to occur. Worst of all, she'd have to relive the hardest, most painful decision she'd ever made in her life. A decision she still knew in her heart was the right one for her son.

But he was too young to understand all that. Only ten years old. His biggest worry should be getting a hit in a Little League game. Not wondering if his birth mother ever really loved him.

Garrett was living proof that those kinds of scars could last a lifetime.

Paul glanced toward the barn. "It's your choice. Play along and leave with me. Otherwise, I'll go straight to Rupert and make him one happy grandpa."

That wasn't a choice, it was a nightmare.

She reached out and grabbed his forearm. "Please. If I ever meant anything to you, don't do this to me."

The bawl of an angry bull pulled her attention away from Paul. She ran to the fence, unhitching the gate just in time for the twelve-hundred-pound Texas long-horn to shoot through it. Rowdy puffed and snorted, shaking his head in the air before making a lap around the corral.

She closed the gate and latched it, aware of the way Garrett was watching her. Then she sensed Paul's presence behind her and tried not to flinch when he laid one hand on her shoulder.

Garrett's eyes narrowed. "I take it you two know each other?"

"As a matter of fact, we do," Paul said, his voice absurdly cheerful. "Mimi is my fiancée."

CHAPTER TWELVE

MIMI SAW a muscle twitch in Garrett's tightly clenched jaw. The shock in his green eyes quickly dissolved into disbelief.

"Your fiancée," he said at last, slowly peeling the leather work gloves off his hands. "Is that right?"

Paul squeezed her shoulder. A painful reminder to play along with his game or he'd destroy her son's life.

Paul smiled. "I want to thank you for giving Mimi an opportunity to play cowgirl for a few weeks. Now she knows what she really wants."

Garrett folded his arms across his chest. "And what is that?"

"Me," Paul replied.

Garrett snorted. "Maybe we should ask the lady her opinion." He turned to Mimi, his voice gentler. "Did you know he was coming?"

"No." Her voice sounded raspy to her ears, and she swallowed hard, trying to think of some way out of this untenable situation. Why hadn't she told Garrett everything when she'd had the chance? Before Paul was here to twist it all out of proportion.

But Mimi knew it didn't matter. She never could have found the right words to make Garrett understand. Not really. She'd been fooling herself, hoping she could erase the past and live for the moment. Lose herself in the fantasy that she and Garrett were the only two people that mattered.

But now it was time to face reality.

"Mimi called me about a week ago, telling me where she was and begging for my forgiveness," Paul said, lying so smoothly it made her sick. "Then she asked me to give her another chance."

Garrett's eyes narrowed on him. "I'll give you one more chance to tell the truth, Renquist, or I'll stop your lies with my fists."

Paul bristled at Garrett's threat. "Touch me and you'll find yourself on the expensive end of a lawsuit."

Mimi was touched by Garrett's faith in her. But then, he was a man who believed in loyalty. A man who had taken her at her word almost from the very beginning.

And how had she repaid him?

She'd lied about her name. Practically forced him into giving her a job. Kept so many secrets. And now she was going to do the worst thing of all—walk out on him. Tears stung her eyes, but she blinked them back.

No matter how much she loved Garrett, she couldn't stay. She couldn't put her child at risk. And would Garrett understand her dilemma, given his feelings about his birth mother? Would he want her anymore? The answer seemed painfully obvious.

Garrett took an ominous step toward Paul, obviously fed up with his games.

"Stop it," she said, stepping between them. She

could see Garrett's hands had formed tight fists, and she knew he was on the verge of losing control.

"Anything for you, darling," Paul said, backing away.

A muscle flicked in Garrett's jaw. "Get the hell off my ranch, Renquist."

"Gladly." Paul held his hand out to Mimi. "Are you ready to go?"

"She's staying," Garrett ordered.

Mimi looked at Garrett, savoring the love smoldering in his eyes. Love for her. She knew she'd never see it there again. Never see *him* again once she made her choice. As if she had a choice. Garrett's feelings for her would change once he knew the truth. He was a man who saw everything in black and white, not grays. A man who wouldn't understand—and could never love—a woman who gave up her own child.

A child Mimi loved. A child who mattered the most at this moment. Despite her feelings for Garrett, she had to make the right decision for her son.

Paul's mouth curved into a sneer. "Perhaps we should ask Miss Casville which man she wants."

Garrett's brows drew together. "Miss *Casville?*"

She squared her shoulders. "That's my name, my real name. Mimi Casville."

He frowned, taking a step closer to her. "Why didn't you tell me?"

"Because I wanted to be anonymous," she said, her voice quiet but strong.

"Mimi is from a very prominent Austin family," Paul interjected. "She's wary of men who just want to use her to get close to all that money and power."

She took a deep breath, her chest so tight she could

hardly breathe. "I'm sorry, Garrett. I never meant for any of this to happen."

A muscle along his jaw flexed. "You're not really going with him?"

"Yes," she said simply, wanting this terrible moment to end.

"Don't worry, hon," Paul said as Garrett stood staring dumbfounded at her. "I'm sure Mr. Lord won't have any trouble finding another ranch hand."

She spun on her heel and hurried toward Paul's car, her strained composure on the edge of crumbling.

"Hold it." Garrett closed the distance between them with three long strides. He grasped Mimi's elbow and whirled her around. "You're not going anywhere until you explain what the hell is going on here."

She licked her lips, her mouth dry as dust. "There's nothing to explain. I'm leaving with Paul. But I want to thank you…"

He dropped her elbow and took a step away from her. "I don't want your gratitude."

"I'm sorry," she said again, her lower lip trembling as he turned away from her. "I know you don't understand, but it's the choice I have to make."

She stared at his broad back and his stiff shoulders. Pride would prevent him from coming after her again.

Paul opened the passenger door for her as Hubert came running around the corner. He stopped long enough to mark a rear tire, then trotted up to her, his stubbed tail wagging as she settled into the leather seat.

Mimi bent down and placed a kiss on top of his

furry head. "Tell Garrett I love him," she whispered, her voice breaking. "I love him so much."

"Get lost, pooch." Paul shoved Hubert away from the car with his foot, then shut the passenger door.

Mimi watched Hubert prance toward Garrett, who stood with his back to the car, one white-knuckled hand curled around a fence post.

Paul settled into the driver's seat, switched on the ignition, then peeled out of the gravel driveway. "Now that we've got that heart-wrenching goodbye scene out of the way, I'll tell you exactly what I want."

GARRETT GRADUALLY became aware of a tugging at his ankle. He glanced down to see Hubert's jaws clamped around the hem of his pant leg. The little dog growled, then pulled on the faded denim with all his might. Garrett reached down and scooped him into his arms. Hubert lapped at his chin with his wet tongue.

"Thanks, boy," he said, wiping dog saliva off his face. "I needed that."

Hubert barked once, then looked at him expectantly.

"Yes, she's really gone." He stared into the corral, watching the massive bull paw at the ground. Wispy white clouds floated in a bright blue sky. A hawk flew high above him, its wings spread wide as it drifted over the south pasture. Garrett had chores to do and cattle to check. This day was the same as any other day on the ranch.

Yet he knew in his heart that nothing would ever really be the same again.

What was it about him that made women want to leave? Last night, Mimi had been warm and loving in his arms. He'd truly believed he'd found his soul mate.

Today, his soul mate had left with another man.

It's the choice I have to make. Her words reverberated in his ears. Obviously, deciding between a rich city slicker and a cowboy who got his hands dirty working the land had been an easy choice for her to make. After spending a few weeks seeing how the other half lived, she'd chosen to let her fiancé whisk her back to a life of luxury.

He set Hubert on the ground, his anger building as he watched the dog chase a butterfly. Hell, he hadn't even known her real last name. A game. She'd been playing a silly game these past few weeks. And playing him for a fool.

Yet she'd found his past for him. Earned his respect as a cowhand. Touched his heart with her concern for a one-hundred-year-old love affair.

It wasn't all a lie. He knew in his bones that Mimi cared about him. But it obviously wasn't enough.

He wasn't as slick or as polished as Paul Renquist. And he definitely didn't move in the Casville social circle. His adoptive parents had left him with a more than comfortable inheritance, but he was determined to make it on his own. He'd never yearned to even rub elbows with the rich and powerful. Or spend any more time in the city than absolutely necessary.

He just wished Mimi had left before he'd fallen in love with her.

Garrett rubbed one hand over his eyes, too exhausted to think clearly. He wanted nothing more than to fall into his bed and surrender to unconsciousness. Then maybe he could block out the memory of Mimi's eyes. Her kisses. Her soft gasps when he touched her in just the right places.

The screech of the hawk brought him back to reality. He watched it swoop down on its prey, then rise again in the sky, a hapless mouse clutched in its powerful claws.

Chores awaited him. Life would go on as it had before. Early mornings and lonely nights. Nothing had really changed.

Garrett Lord had survived without Mimi before. He'd damn well find a way to do it again.

"THIS IS IT." Paul hesitated outside the door to Rupert Casville's study. "Can you at least smile or something? You hardly look like a blushing bride-to-be."

Mimi stared at him, unable to conceal her disgust. "You're blackmailing me into marrying you. What exactly do I have to smile about?"

"I think the arrangement I proposed is more than fair. We'll have a marriage in name only in exchange for no prenuptial agreement."

She looked at him. "Money? Is that the only reason you're going to all this trouble?"

"Of course not." He gave her a wry smile. "I happen to find you irresistible."

She turned toward the door. "Let's just get this over with."

"Let me do most of the talking," Paul admonished. "I already called your father this morning and told him you were coming home. He doesn't know you found out about his incentive program. And I think it's best if we keep it that way.''

Mimi arched a brow. "Best for whom?"

"Little Joshua, of course."

Apprehension skittered over her skin. "This isn't going to work. My father isn't a stupid man. He'll want to know why I've been gone so long."

"I've already handled it."

"How?"

"I simply confirmed his suspicions that you came down with a case of cold feet and were staying with an old college friend because you were so embarrassed."

"He bought that?"

"Of course." Paul smiled. "I think you're underestimating his desire for a grandchild. Questions and doubts might cause a delay. He wants nothing more than for us to be married as soon as possible."

She tilted her head at him. "And what do you want? It's more than just money. It has to be."

"You're right. It's something that's eluded me all my life. Something that people don't give to the son of an alcoholic father and a mother who makes her living cleaning public rest rooms." He squared his shoulders. "I want respect."

"You can't buy respect, Paul. You have to earn it."

He snorted. "That's a good one, coming from you. What have you ever had to earn?"

She knew the answer, though she didn't voice it. Garrett's love. Garrett's respect. She'd won both in a few short weeks. And lost them both in just one day.

"Marrying into the Casville family will give me

the respect I deserve," he continued, straightening his tie. "Paul Renquist will finally be somebody."

"This isn't the way, Paul." She found herself almost feeling sorry for him. "It's not too late to walk away."

"Yes, it is." He opened the door to the study. "Look who I found, Rupert."

Her father looked up from his desk, then dropped the pen in his hand. "Mimi."

Her throat tightened. Despite his betrayal, he was still her father, and she loved him. "Hello, Dad."

"Hello, Dad?" He rose slowly to his feet, then rounded the desk. "Is that all you have to say to me? How about a hug?"

Mimi walked into his arms, inhaling the familiar bay rum scent of his aftershave. He seemed thinner than before, and a little grayer. She closed her eyes as he held her tight.

The urge to tell him everything was almost overwhelming. But would that help matters or only make them ten times worse? For her son, Mimi knew she simply couldn't take that kind of risk.

"I've missed you," he whispered against her hair.

"I've missed you, too," she replied, and meant it.

Paul cleared his throat, effectively ending their hug. "Mimi and I have some wonderful news."

Rupert held her at arm's length. "You do?"

Paul came up behind her and circled his arm around her waist. "We plan to be married this Saturday."

"That's wonderful!"

Mimi's heart sank at her father's delighted expression. Paul was right. Her father was too caught up in his obsession with having a grandchild to question her abrupt return. Probably because he was afraid to hear the reasons she'd left.

Rupert rubbed his hands together. "Five days isn't very long. We'll have to call the caterers and contact all the guests."

"No," she said abruptly, then steadied herself. "I want something simple this time. Just family."

Paul walked up behind her. "I told Mimi she could have whatever she wanted."

"Of course." Rupert smiled at his daughter. "Whatever makes you happy."

"There's something else," Mimi said, anxious to escape to the refuge of her room. She needed time to think. Time to figure some way out of this mess. "I don't want Paul to sign a prenuptial agreement this time. It's...very important to me."

Rupert frowned. "That's ridiculous."

"It's the only way I'll marry him."

Paul looked sheepish. "Turns out that last prenuptial agreement was part of the problem, Rupert. Mimi didn't think it was very romantic."

Rupert's gaze centered on his daughter. "I think we should talk about this."

Mimi didn't have the strength to argue with him. Her stomach was twisted in knots from all the lies, and her head ached. "I'm very tired. I think I need to go lie down for a while."

Rupert shook his head. "But you haven't even told me where you've been all this time. Or what you've been doing. I was worried sick about you."

"I'll fill you in on the details, Rupert," Paul said as Mimi turned and hastily left the room. She closed the door behind her, effectively shutting out the sound of her fiancé's voice.

Her fiancé.

Mimi leaned her head against the door and closed her eyes. "Oh, Garrett, what am I going to do now?"

THREE DAYS LATER, Garrett sat at his kitchen table with Shelby, Lana, and Michael. "So that's it," he said. "The history of the Larrimore family. *Our* family."

His three siblings silently stared at the documents spread across the table. Lana had the Calloway centennial book open in front of her. She looked at Garrett, tears gleaming in her eyes. "This is incredible. I feel like I found a small piece of myself that I didn't know was missing." She pointed to the photograph. "I can see Michael in this little boy."

"Our grandfather." Shelby leaned over to study the picture. "Hans Larrimore."

"Our name is Larrimore," Michael said, shaking his head in wonderment. "And we're part German."

Shelby picked up Garrett's teddy bear off the table. "Can you believe this toy belonged to our grandfather? And our father."

"Gary Larrimore," Lana said, rolling their father's name around on her tongue. "I wonder if you're named after him, Garrett."

"We'll never know," he said quietly. "Until we find her."

He didn't have to explain who he meant. The room grew quiet again as all three of them thought about the mother they didn't remember. The woman who had left them on the steps of Maitland Maternity twenty-five years ago.

"Maybe this is enough," Shelby said softly, still holding the teddy bear in her hands. "Maybe we should respect her wishes and leave her alone."

Garrett slammed his hand on the table. "No!"

All three of them jumped. Michael scowled at him. "What the hell is wrong with you?"

Garrett stood up, his chair scraping across the floor. "What about our wishes? What about what we want? Don't our feelings matter?"

"You don't have to yell," Shelby snapped, setting the teddy bear on the table.

Michael rested his chin on his steepled fingers. "I suppose we could hire a private detective to go to Sagebrush County. There's a chance that someone in the area might know something about LeeAnn Larrimore."

"I'll go there myself," Garrett said, walking to the window. He'd looked out the window many times in the last three days. Too many times. Mimi wasn't coming back. It was time he accepted it and put her out of his mind.

"I still don't think we should rush into anything." Shelby glanced at her watch. "Look, I know we've got a lot of decisions to make but I was supposed to meet Gray at the diner twenty minutes ago. How about supper at my house on Sunday? We can discuss it more then."

Michael nodded. "Jenny and I will be there. I think Dylan and Gray should be there, too. This concerns all of us."

Shelby picked up the book. "Can I take this with

me? I'd like to read it again. Give it a chance to really soak in this time."

"Sure," Lana said, then looked at her oldest brother. "You don't mind, do you, Garrett?"

He turned away from the window, deeply regretting his earlier outburst. "Of course not. Take anything you want."

"Where did you get all this stuff, anyway?" Michael picked up their father's birth certificate. "I meant to ask you before, but I got too wrapped up in discovering the long-lost Larrimores."

"Mimi found it." It was the first time he'd spoken her name aloud since she'd left.

"Mimi?" Michael grinned. "Hey, is that the new ranch hand Lana was telling us about? I've got to meet her."

"She's not here," he replied in a clipped voice.

Lana stood up. "It's getting late, and you probably have chores to do."

Shelby walked toward the door. "I'll expect everyone on Sunday. Six o'clock sharp."

"Shelby," Garrett called as she opened the back door. He walked to her and placed a kiss on her forehead. "Sorry I yelled."

She smiled at him, then reached out to squeeze his hand. "Forgiven."

Michael left shortly after Shelby, but Lana lingered in the kitchen.

"Do you want to stay for supper?" Garrett opened the refrigerator door and perused the contents. "I've got salami sandwiches on the menu."

"Maybe next time. Dylan is expecting me home

soon." Lana fidgeted with the Bruner Bear, setting it on the table, then picking it up again.

Garrett closed the refrigerator door. "Is something wrong?"

"You tell me."

He folded his arms across his chest, determined not to spill his pathetic story to his little sister. "I'm fine."

"So that's why you blew up tonight?"

He frowned. "I already apologized for that."

"I'm worried about you, Garrett." She moved closer to him. "You look terrible. You haven't shaved and the kitchen sink is full of dirty dishes."

"This from a woman who didn't own a vacuum for over a year."

"That was when I was a student," she explained in her own defense. "Besides, my next-door neighbor let me use hers."

"I suppose I could buy a dishwasher," Garrett mused.

She narrowed her eyes. "Stop trying to change the subject."

"You were the one who brought up the dirty dishes."

"And I guess I'm going to have to be the one to bring up Mimi, too." She grabbed her purse off the back of a kitchen chair and reached inside. Then she held up a small newspaper clipping. "Did you see Bettina Collingsworth's latest column?"

He stared at the picture of Mimi. The black and white photograph didn't begin to do justice to her beauty. The headline hit him like a kick in the gut.

Casville Heiress to Marry Saturday.

He read the item silently, each word burning into his brain.

Mimi Casville, the fugitive fiancée of attorney Paul Renquist, is reportedly ready to attempt another trip down the aisle. A small, intimate family wedding is planned. Sources say the bride will wear a simple silk chiffon tea-length gown with Alencon lace accenting the collar and cuffs.

Garrett closed his eyes, unable to bear reading any more.

"I don't understand any of this," Lana said. "I thought her name was Banyon."

He tossed the newspaper clipping onto the counter. "Apparently, she didn't want anyone to know about her connection to Rupert Casville."

Her brow furrowed. "Well, whatever her name is, you two seemed so right for each other the night of the barbecue. And the way she looked at you, Garrett." Lana shook her head. "It's not the way a woman should look at a man when she's planning to marry someone else in less than a month!"

"I don't want to talk about Mimi."

"Good. Because I think this calls for action, not words."

He arched a brow. "What exactly do you have in mind?"

"Go to her. Find out if this marriage is what she really wants."

"Mimi made her feelings quite clear when she rode off this ranch with her fiancé."

Lana met his gaze. "Look, big brother, don't take this the wrong way, but you're not the best judge of women."

"Obviously."

"That's not what I mean," she replied. "You always see everything in black and white. But sometimes we can get lost in a sea of gray. That almost happened to me and Dylan. I'd hate to see it happen to you and Mimi."

"You hardly even know her."

Lana tipped up her chin. "I know she's the woman who found the past you've been searching for so desperately. I hear the longing in your voice whenever you say her name. And I can see what living without her for just a few short days has done to you."

Garrett could feel the heat burn in his cheeks. Had his feelings for Mimi been that obvious? "What the hell do you want me to do? Beg her to come back to me?"

"How about just telling Mimi you love her?"

He raked one hand through his hair. "But I'm not the man she wants. I'm not a graduate of some fancy Ivy League university. I drive cattle instead of a Jaguar. I'm more familiar with manure than caviar." He emitted a mirthless laugh. "I'd no more fit into her world than she'd fit into mine."

"So you're just going to let her go?"

"She's the one who left." He bit the words out more sharply than he'd intended.

Lana didn't say anything for a moment. Then she

reached out and gently touched his arm. "Sometimes people leave because they feel they don't have any other choice. I truly believe that's why our birth mother left us on that doorstep. The point is, you're not a helpless two-year-old anymore. You don't have to just watch Mimi walk away."

"It's not that simple," he said softly.

"Only because you're too stubborn and proud to make it simple." Lana sighed, then she reached up to kiss his cheek. "I need to go. Just please think about what I said."

Garrett didn't say anything. Instead he gave her a warm hug, then walked her to her car. But when he returned to the house, he couldn't keep from picking up the news clipping once more. Mimi looked different to him somehow. Remote. A world away.

Too far away to find her way back to him again.

CHAPTER THIRTEEN

MIMI STOOD ALONE in the anteroom of the chapel, watching the old wall clock silently tick down the last precious seconds of her freedom.

She wore a simple ivory dress with matching pumps, and no veil or jewelry. This wedding might be a sham, but she refused to masquerade as a blushing bride.

Thankfully, she'd convinced her father to invite only immediate family the second time around. He'd insisted on a small reception at the house, though, so she'd have to keep up the pretense for at least an hour after the ceremony.

She closed her eyes, reminiscing about how she'd spent another Saturday night. Garrett had cooked a spaghetti dinner, then they'd taken a moonlit ride to the south pasture to check the cattle. She remembered the way the breeze had ruffled his hair, and how straight and tall he'd sat in the saddle.

"Don't do this," Mimi ordered herself, then opened her eyes. Dreaming about Garrett Lord wouldn't make this any easier. Just the opposite. It almost made her forget the reason, the very important reason, for going through with this wedding. Almost made her give in to the overwhelming temptation to kick off her high-heeled shoes and make a run for it.

A knock at the door put an end to her escape fantasy. Rupert stuck his head inside. "It's almost time."

She took a deep breath. "I'm ready."

She joined her father in the hallway, took his arm, and they walked silently toward the sanctuary. Sunlight streamed from the double glass doors of the chapel, and she could see Paul inside, waiting for her at the end of the long aisle. A middle-aged woman sat by the door, strumming softly on a harp.

Rupert gently squeezed her forearm. "This is it."

Panic seized her, and she fought the urge to scream.

Her father took one step down the aisle, but Mimi couldn't move. She let go of his arm, then grabbed the door frame to steady herself.

"Wait," she gasped, trying desperately to regain her equilibrium. "Just give me a moment."

Rupert frowned, then whispered, "Don't you think Paul has waited long enough?"

"No," said a deep voice behind them. "Not nearly long enough."

Mimi whirled. "Garrett!"

Garrett nodded toward her father. "Will you excuse us?" Then he turned to Mimi and swept her up in his arms. "We need to talk."

"No, Garrett," she cried as he carried her toward the door. "I have to marry him."

"Hey," Paul shouted from inside the chapel, "what the hell is going on here?"

But Garrett didn't stick around long enough to give him an answer. With Rupert still sputtering behind them, he walked briskly out of the chapel and down the long row of steps.

Mimi blinked when she saw his horse tethered to

the handrail. "You rode Brutus all the way into Austin?"

"I thought we might need a quick getaway." Garrett lifted her into the saddle, then loosened the reins.

The chapel door slammed open, and Paul strode down the steps two at a time, her father close behind him. But they were too late. Garrett swung up behind her and spurred the horse into a gallop. He held the reins in one hand. His other hand was firmly around her waist, keeping her safe.

Tears stung her eyes as they raced away from the chapel. She'd dreamed of some type of rescue every night for the past week. But this was only a short reprieve. She couldn't afford to run away again.

Not at the expense of her child.

"I have to go back," she shouted, but either the wind or the noise of the traffic or his own stubbornness prevented him from hearing her.

They were several blocks from the chapel when Garrett finally slowed his horse. A pristine brick building stood before them, surrounded by a lush blanket of green grass and several trees.

Garrett helped Mimi off the horse, then jumped down, loosely wrapping the horse's reins around a low branch of a nearby pecan tree.

Mimi read the sign at the front of the building, then turned to Garrett. "The Maitland Maternity Clinic?"

"That's right." He grabbed her hand and led her to the front step. "This is where Megan Maitland found me and my brother and sisters, with nothing but our first names and a note from our mother asking her to find us a good home."

She looked at him. "Why did you bring me here?"

"Twenty-five years ago the most important woman in my life abandoned me. I didn't know why then, and I may never know. But I refuse to let it happen twice in one lifetime." He moved closer to her, grabbing both her hands in his own. "I love you, Mimi Casville. I can't offer you a fancy house or a ritzy lifestyle, but I'll give you everything I have. Except my heart. That you already own."

Tears spilled over her cheeks as she slowly shook her head. "I don't want to love you, Garrett, but I do. More than you'll ever know. I wish I didn't love you. I wish I'd never met you!"

Garrett tenderly brushed a stray curl off her cheek. "I don't think it was an accident that you showed up in my hayloft. I think it was fate. Now you just need to follow your heart."

"Like Katherine MacGuire?" Mimi took a deep, shuddering breath. "She followed her heart, and looked what happened. She never came back."

"A good thing, too."

Mimi blanched. "What?"

"I discovered the rest of her story. Katherine MacGuire ran away from home, planning to marry Boyd Harrison. But she never found him. Instead, she fell in love with another man on the long journey to San Antonio. A man named Wilhelm Larrimore."

Her eyes widened. "You mean…"

He nodded. "Katherine 'Kate' MacGuire Larrimore was my great-grandmother. The woman in the picture with the freckles and the six children."

"I don't believe it," she breathed.

"I found their marriage certificate among all those documents you brought me, then did a little research of my own. Katherine never came back for her journal because her parents were evicted from the property shortly after she ran away. They ended up settling somewhere near Laredo."

He took a step closer to her. "Don't you see, Mimi? Katherine was never meant to marry Boyd. But if she hadn't met him, she and Wilhelm probably never would have found each other."

"Just like if I'd never met Paul, I wouldn't have found you." Mimi leaned against the brick building, her eyes hot and tired. She wondered briefly if it was already too late. Had Paul sold his secret? "I have to go back."

"I know you love me." A muscle flexed in Garrett's jaw. "So tell me why you insist on marrying Renquist."

She looked into his eyes. "Because my child's life depends on it."

The door to Maitland Maternity opened, and a very pregnant woman waddled out, one hand pressed against the small of her back. She stared for a moment at the two of them, then at Brutus grazing on the front lawn.

"Come with me," he said, pulling Mimi away from the entrance of the clinic. He stopped under a shady willow tree that concealed them from prying eyes.

"Tell me everything," Garrett said, not touching her, but standing close enough that she could see the faint sun lines at the corners of his eyes and the shadow of beard on his jawline.

"I became pregnant when I was eighteen years old and a freshman in college," she began, finally releasing the secret she'd kept buried inside of her for all these years. "The first time my boyfriend and I were together, we didn't use birth control. We were too caught up in the romance of the moment. But I soon found out that once is all it takes. Unfortunately, we were both too young and naive to realize that sometimes the consequences of our actions can last a lifetime."

She looked at him, unable to read his implacable expression. "Anyway, by the time I was sure I was pregnant, my boyfriend was in Europe for the semester as part of a student exchange program. I thought he loved me, but all my letters and telephone calls to him went unanswered."

"He didn't want the baby?" Garrett asked.

"He didn't even know about it. He was killed in an automobile accident in London before I ever got a chance to tell him. By then I was four months pregnant and definitely starting to panic. I decided to tell my father, since it would be impossible to hide my pregnancy from him much longer."

Mimi closed her eyes, remembering that warm day in March. They'd gone together to the cemetery to put daffodils on her mother's grave. "I told him everything. Then I cried on his shoulder and told him I didn't know what to do. He insisted I get an abortion."

Her throat grew tight at the memory. "I knew that wasn't the choice for me, but when I suggested adoption, my father exploded. He told me he'd never let

some stranger raise a Casville. He vowed to raise the
baby himself before he ever let that happen. Back then
I believed my father had the power to do anything he
wanted. Sometimes I still do.''

Something flashed in Garrett's eyes, and it spurred
her onward. ''Yes, my baby could have had the Casville money. The Casville name. The Casville heritage. But at what cost?''

She sucked in a huge breath. ''I grew up in a forty-
room mansion, but most of the time I was alone. The
cook fed me and the housekeeper baby-sat me while
my father worked late at the office. Even before my
mother died, their social calendar kept them too busy
to spend much time with me.''

She repeated the phrase she'd heard her father utter
so often while she was growing up. '''When you're
a Casville, you have an image to maintain.'''

She smiled through her tears. ''You know how little
girls sometimes dream they're really a princess and
someone switched them at birth?'' She didn't wait for
him to reply. ''Well, I used to dream I was really the
cook's daughter and that someone had switched me
at birth. That's when I first became interested in genealogy. I wanted to research the Casville family tree,
because I was certain I'd find a mistake somewhere
in there.''

Her legs gave way, and she slid onto the grass.
Garrett took off his cowboy hat and sat beside her,
his back against the tree.

''I wanted a different life for my baby,'' she said
softly. ''I was only eighteen and knew nothing about
children. Even worse, I knew my father would take

over. Raise the baby in his own image. He'd probably start by sending my child away to some fancy private boarding school.''

She swallowed hard. "I didn't want that. I wanted him to have two parents who would love him more than life itself. A father to take him camping and teach him baseball. A mother to read him bedtime stories and kiss all his worries away. A normal family. A happy childhood.''

She hesitated, but Garrett didn't say anything. The first frissons of apprehension skittered up her spine. "One of my favorite college professors had been desperately trying to have a baby with her husband for several years. It was common knowledge around campus. So I asked her if she wanted mine. We arranged a private adoption.''

She turned toward him. "Even now, I don't regret my decision. Joshua was born on August 26, 1991. I had to have a Cesarean section, but he was perfect.'' She closed her eyes, the image of her baby so clear in her mind. "Beautiful.''

She took a deep breath. "I spent the summer in France with my college professor and her husband during the last trimester of my pregnancy. Bill and Dena are wonderful people. They were at the hospital in Paris when Joshua was born. Dena held him before I did.'' Her throat tightened. "But I kissed him goodbye. And I told him that I loved him.''

Garrett reached out and brushed the wetness off her cheek. "What does all this have to do with your marrying Renquist?''

"I showed up in your hayloft after I found out that

Paul was being paid to marry me." She looked at Garrett. "Now he knows about Joshua, and he's threatened to tell my father. Threatened to turn my son's happy life upside down unless I go through with the wedding."

Garrett's brow furled. "Your father still doesn't know about the baby?"

She shook her head. "I told him I'd had the abortion in France. It's the only time in my life I've ever lied to him." She looked into Garrett's eyes. "He never knew the truth. But after he was diagnosed with cancer two years ago, he began to talk about the baby. Wishing he'd encouraged me to keep it. He's become obsessed with having grandchildren. Especially a male heir to carry on the Casville legacy. If he knew about Joshua…" Her voice trailed off.

"Are you saying he'd really try to take him away from his adoptive parents?"

"I don't know," she replied honestly. "But can I take that chance? And what if it comes down to me choosing sides? Would my son understand why I believe he should stay with his adopted parents? Or would he think I was just rejecting him? Again."

"Does he think that now?" Garrett asked softly.

"I hope not. His parents planned to tell him the truth about his adoption from the beginning, even before he was old enough to fully understand." She wiped away the last of her tears. "They've got pictures of me, and I gave them a complete family history. Probably much more than the poor kid will want to know."

Garrett smiled at that.

"They'll tell him anything he wants to know as soon as he wants to know it. *If* he wants to know it. And in his own good time. Not mine. Not my father's."

"So you were willing to marry a man you didn't love to protect your son?"

"Yes." She tipped up her chin. "I still am."

He scowled. "Like hell."

She turned toward him, resisting the urge to wrap her arms around him. If she didn't stay strong now, she'd crumble completely later. "Don't you understand, Garrett? I love my son too much to let him get hurt."

"And I love you too much to let you go."

A spark of hope flared inside her. "Can you possibly wait for me? My marriage to Paul will be in name only. He's even hinted that he might be willing to get a divorce after a year or two. Especially with no prenuptial agreement."

"And you believe him?"

He'd raised her unvoiced fears. The ones that had kept her awake at night. What if Paul decided he didn't want a divorce? What if this nightmare went on and on? "What else can I do?"

Garrett reached for her hand.

"Believe in us."

PAUL MADE UP his mind by the time he reached the Casville estate. He sat in the driver's seat of his Jaguar, impatiently waiting for Rupert's black Lexus to clear the gate. Then he pulled in behind him, mentally composing his best sales speech. The information he had to sell should be worth a least a million dollars. But first, he'd have to entice the old tightwad to choke up that much money.

Especially since Rupert was convinced his daughter had just been kidnapped by some crazed cowboy. Paul emitted a derisive snort as he pulled into the circular drive, then cut the engine. Hadn't Rupert noticed that Mimi wasn't fighting her abductor? Hadn't he seen the relief in her eyes?

"To hell with her," Paul muttered, climbing out of his car and slamming the door behind him. She could ride off into the sunset with Howdy Doody for all he cared. Paul Renquist was still going to come out a winner.

He walked into the house and almost bumped into Rupert, who stood frozen in the doorway of his study. One glimpse at Rupert's stunned expression told him the game might not be over, after all.

Mimi sat behind Rupert's desk.

"Thank God," Rupert exclaimed, walking into the study. "I thought you'd been kidnapped. I was just about to call the police."

"That still might be a good idea," she said, her gaze fixed on Paul.

He walked through the open door, ignoring her threat. For the past week, he'd seen the fear reflected in her eyes. Fear he'd put there. And he'd relished the power it gave him. Now he wanted to see it there again. To wipe that confident expression off her beautiful face.

"I don't think we'll need the police," Paul said as he ambled into the study, "but your father might want to consult a good lawyer. One who specializes in child custody cases.''

Rupert looked between the two of them. ''What the hell is going on here?''

Paul smiled. ''More than you know at the moment, Rupert.''

Mimi folded her hands together. ''Go ahead, Paul. Tell him.''

''Tell me what?'' Rupert demanded.

Paul met her gaze. He knew she was bluffing. She *had* to be bluffing. ''Your daughter's been keeping a secret from you, Rupert.''

He waited for the fear to flash in her blue eyes. But she just stared at him, her expression as serene as it had been the moment he'd walked into the study.

Doubt gnawed at him. But he couldn't back down. Not with one million reasons to stay in the game. He turned toward Rupert. ''She'll never tell you, but I will. For a price.''

Adrenaline pumped through his blood. Like the high he used to get from his first martini of the day. Power. He'd fed off it since giving up the booze. Not a perfect replacement, but definitely addictive.

Rupert walked to the bar and poured himself a whiskey. Then he turned to his daughter. ''Let's start at the beginning. Who was that man who abducted you from the wedding?''

She stood and walked to her father, taking the drink out of his hand. ''His name is Garrett Lord.'' She went to the bar and tossed the whiskey into the sink. ''And you know that stuff isn't good for you.''

Rupert sighed. ''I thought maybe I was too sober

for all of this to make sense." He settled into a leather armchair. "Who is Garrett Lord?"

"The man who found me in his hayloft after I ran out of the first wedding. It might interest you to know that I overheard you and Paul talking about your incentive program shortly before the ceremony was due to start."

Rupert paled. "Mimi, I—"

She held her hand in the air. "It doesn't matter anymore."

Her father frowned. "You've been living with this Lord fellow all this time?"

"Yes." Her voice softened. "And falling in love with him."

"What about Paul?"

"Paul tracked me down at Garrett's ranch and blackmailed me into marrying him."

Paul stepped forward, all too aware that the situation was slipping out of his control. If Mimi turned Rupert against him, he'd lose everything. Time to play his trump card. "Rupert, there's something else you should know. Something important."

"No," Mimi said sharply. "Let me." Then she squared her shoulders and faced her father. "Dad, you have a grandson."

MIMI HELD her breath, waiting for her father's reaction. Rupert just stared at her, his mouth working, but no words came out.

At last, he turned to Paul. "I want to talk to my daughter alone."

Paul glanced at Mimi, then at Rupert. "But—"

"Get the hell out of here!" Rupert ordered.

Mimi held her breath, fearing the situation could get ugly if Paul stayed and tried to drive a wedge between them. But at last he turned on his heel and left the study.

Rupert walked toward the door, his shoulders stiff. He closed it, then stood for a moment with his back to her. At last he turned, his face looking older and grayer than before. "You had the baby."

"Yes."

He closed his eyes. "I really need a whiskey."

"I really need you to listen to me," she replied, her voice tight. "For once."

Then she told him everything. Rupert's shoulders sagged as her story unfolded, but he didn't interrupt. Didn't lose his temper, as she'd half expected. When she finally finished, she felt drained. But for the first time in over ten years, there were no secrets between them.

"A grandson," Rupert said softly, sagging onto the leather sofa. "I have a grandson."

"His name is Joshua," Mimi said, walking to her father and seating herself beside him on the sofa. "He's ten years old. But you're a stranger to him. And so am I."

He looked at her. "Why didn't you ever tell me?"

"Because I was afraid."

He frowned. "Afraid of what? I love you, Mimi, no matter what. I never would have blamed you or disowned you."

"No, Dad," she interjected, "I was afraid you wouldn't listen to me. I knew adoption was the right choice for me. I knew it in my heart then, and I know it now.''

''But I could have raised that boy right! I could have given him every advantage.'' Hope flared in his faded brown eyes. ''I still can.''

''See?'' she challenged, reaching for his big hand, softened with wrinkles. ''You're still not listening. It was *my* choice. I won't let you disrupt his life.''

He squeezed her hand. ''But a grandson! I've always wanted a grandson.''

''I know.'' She took a deep breath. ''And I plan to give you lots of grandchildren. But on one condition.''

His gaze grew wary. ''What condition?''

''You'll leave Joshua and his parents completely alone. Or else you'll never see me again. Or any of your future grandchildren.''

He arched one grizzled brow. ''Is that a threat?''

''It's a promise.''

He sighed. ''You've become as tough a negotiator as your old man.''

''Do we have a deal?''

He stood up and walked to the open French doors. He stared outside for a long moment, then turned to face her. ''Mimi, I'll never forgive myself for paying Paul to marry you. I should have realized how unhappy you were when you ran away from the wedding. Then I fooled myself into thinking you came back because you truly did love Paul. I never knew he was blackmailing you.''

''I know, Dad,'' she said gently.

''If never knowing Joshua…'' His voice cracked,

and he took a deep, shuddering breath. "If that is my penance, then so be it."

Hope flared inside her. "Really?"

For the first time in her life, she saw her father's eyes fill with tears. She'd never seen him cry before, not even at her mother's funeral.

"Facing death does funny things to a man," Rupert began. "Makes him realize he's not in control of his own destiny. I couldn't accept that, so I tried to control the people around me. Including the daughter I love more than life itself." He walked to her. "I don't want to lose you, Mimi—even though I couldn't blame you if you never wanted to see me again. If you're willing to give me a second chance, I'm more than ready to take it."

Mimi stood and held out her hand. "Shall we shake on it?"

He grabbed her hand, then pulled her into his arms for a hug that left her breathless.

"I love you, Dad," she whispered.

"I love you, too," he said gruffly. "Now, when do I get those grandchildren you mentioned?"

She laughed as she stepped out of his embrace. "I'd better find myself a husband first."

He narrowed his eyes. "From the way that Lord fellow was looking at you, I'd say there's a good chance I've got a grandchild already on the way. Maybe I'd better find my shotgun."

A blush burned her cheeks. "Forget the shotgun and find a telephone instead. I want you to call Bettina Collingsworth."

He scowled. ''That gossip columnist? Why would I possibly want to talk to her?''

''Because I'm going to give her an exclusive on my wedding, provided she agrees to do me a small favor.''

''What kind of favor?''

''You'll see.'' She smiled, then headed toward the door. ''Just tell her to contact me as soon as possible.''

''Where are you going?''

''I've got to hunt down a groom.''

CHAPTER FOURTEEN

PAUL PACED outside Rupert's study, frantically trying to come up with a contingency plan. It was entirely possible Mimi might hold something back. The boy's name or location, for instance. That information had to be worth something to Rupert. Not a million dollars, of course, but perhaps a hundred thousand?

The study door opened, and Rupert waved him inside. "Come in, Paul. We need to talk."

His legs shook slightly as he followed Rupert into the study. He was surprised to find Mimi already gone, and assumed she'd left through the French doors leading out to the garden. Perhaps old man Casville had kicked her butt out of the house. No doubt he was pretty steamed by her duplicity.

Given this new turn of events, Paul reconsidered his strategy. Perhaps one million had been too conservative. He'd start his asking price at a million, then negotiate from there.

"Have a seat," Rupert said, moving behind his desk. His checkbook lay open in front of him.

Paul picked the chair nearest the desk. He could see that the top check was already made out and signed. The number of zeros on it made his heart skip a beat.

"My daughter has told me some very disturbing

news,'' Rupert began, neatly separating the signed check from the checkbook along the perforation.

Paul's pulse picked up. ''It must have come as quite a shock to you.''

''You can't even begin to imagine how I feel.''

Paul leaned back in his chair, not wanting to appear too eager. ''Curious, I expect. And I'll be more than happy to satisfy that curiosity.''

''Curious?'' Rupert shook his head. ''No. Furious would be more accurate. Furious with myself for allowing a snake like you near my daughter. And furious with you for having the nerve to blackmail her.''

Paul sat up. ''But—''

''Shut up!'' Rupert roared. ''Now, I'm going to talk nice and slow so you understand.'' He held up the check. ''This goes to my lawyer, my *new* lawyer, in a sealed envelope, along with a letter. If anything happens to my daughter or to Joshua, if you even so much as cause one of them to break a fingernail, then that letter gets delivered.''

Paul tried to breathe, but he couldn't seem to suck any air into his lungs.

''Don't you want to know what's in the letter?'' Rupert didn't wait for him to respond. ''Detailed instructions to a certain man, a mercenary, who will be more than happy to break your arms, your legs and any other appendages I deem appropriate.''

Rupert waved the check in the air. ''This is double his usual fee, so I know he'll be eager to perform the job to my satisfaction.''

Paul swallowed hard. ''I think I understand perfectly.''

''Wonderful. Now about this information you have

for me.'' Rupert placed his steepled fingers under his
grizzled chin. ''I hope you were going to tell me that
you plan to leave the country soon. Permanently.
South America, perhaps? Or Europe?''

Paul gave a jerky nod.

''Good.'' Rupert leaned back in his chair. ''I think
you'll be happier there, Paul. And much safer.''

GARRETT PICKED UP the telephone receiver to check
for a dial tone. The phone was still working. So why
hadn't Mimi called yet?

He paced back and forth across the braided rug in
his living room, a fire crackling in the hearth. She'd
left for her father's house a lifetime ago. He checked
his watch. Three hours, to be exact.

So where was she now?

His stomach twisted as the worst possibility came
to mind. Maybe her father or Renquist had convinced
her to go through with the ceremony. Maybe she was
already married.

''Hell,'' he muttered, thrusting one hand through
his hair. He never should have let Mimi face her father alone, even if she had insisted on it. He walked
impatiently to the window, but the driveway was still
empty. He vaguely noted that Hubert had finally
stopped barking at the coyotes.

A sound at the front door made his heart leap, then
he recognized it as Hubert's characteristic scratching.
He moved toward the door, wondering if he should
drive into Austin and look for Mimi. He turned the
doorknob and opened it far enough for the little dog
to scamper inside, his toenails clicking on the hardwood floor.

Hubert headed straight for his dog dish. His empty dog dish.

"Sorry, boy," Garrett said, walking into the kitchen and retrieving a bag of dog food from the cupboard underneath the sink. "I forgot about supper."

Hubert sat in front of his dog dish, waiting patiently for Garrett to serve him.

That's when he saw it. Clipped to Hubert's collar was a small scroll of paper, tied with a red bow. He dumped the dry dog food kernels into the bowl, spilling half of them onto the floor. Then he dropped the bag and untied the bow.

The notepaper unfurled in his hand, and he read one simple sentence.

Meet me in the hayloft.

Grinning, Garrett stuffed the note into his shirt pocket, then sprinted for the door. By the time he got to the barn, his heart was beating double time in his chest. A horse whinnied, then quieted. He reached the ladder leading to the hayloft in four long strides. He grabbed a plank rung, then climbed up the ladder, one hand over the other.

"About time you got here, cowboy."

He turned to see Mimi smiling at him. She was perched on a bale of straw wearing a simple white wedding dress that outlined her hourglass figure, then flared at her hips. At her bare feet lay a large blue blanket over a thick mattress of loose straw.

A bottle of champagne sat chilling in a tin bucket of ice nearby. Right next to a CD player emitting a sultry, lilting tune.

He stared at the blanket for a moment, his body

instantly responding to the silent invitation, then he looked at Mimi. He stood there a moment, drinking in the sight of her. His fears of never seeing her again melted away in the warmth of her smile.

She arched a blond brow. "Do you want to know why there's a bride in your barn?"

"I do."

She smiled. "Now there's an interesting choice of words. I don't suppose you'd want to repeat them. Say in front of a minister?"

He looked around the loft. "Did you bring one with you?"

"No." She nibbled her bottom lip. "Actually, if you want me to be honest with you…"

"Always," he interjected.

She cleared her throat. "I told my father that he'd be having grandchildren. Soon. Now, I know we haven't even discussed marriage…"

"Then let's remedy that right now." He reached into his shirt pocket and pulled out the diamond ring he'd bought just a few short hours ago. Then he fell to one knee, reaching for her left hand and sliding the ring smoothly onto her fourth finger. It fit perfectly.

"Mimi Banyon Casville," he said solemnly, "will you marry me?"

"I thought you'd never ask!" She threw her arms around his neck, and they both tumbled backward onto the blanket.

"I take it that's a yes," he said, laughing as he lay flat on his back.

"Definitely a yes." She sat up and straddled his waist. "Now I've got you exactly where I want you."

Garrett's body tightened, and when he spoke, his voice was low and husky.

"The question is, what are you going to do with me?"

She reached down and began unbuttoning his shirt. "Everything."

EPILOGUE

Three months later

JOURNALISTS FLANKED both sides of the cathedral, cameras in hand, as they waited for Austin's own runaway bride to come barreling out of the church. After all, Mimi Casville had made headlines with two botched marriage attempts already. Of course, this wasn't the same groom. But a marriage between one of the richest heiresses in Texas and a cowboy?

Not one of the cynical reporters there believed she'd go through with it. The *Austin American Statesman* had even run a poll and published it in yesterday's edition, with people voting two-to-one that the bride would make a run for it.

Two television vans, one staked out in front of the cathedral and one staked out in the back, let the engines idle so they could give chase when she made her escape.

The sanctuary itself was standing room only. Not one of the two hundred invited guests had turned down the invitation. Many of them were Maitlands, with spouses and children in tow. The family had grown large enough to take up a good portion of pew space. But none of the reporters had been allowed inside. So they waited outside, idly chattering as the minutes ticked by.

A sudden commotion at the double glass doors of the cathedral brought them all to attention. A bride in a long white gown, her face covered by a lacy veil, flew out of the church. She raced down the concrete steps two at a time, her voluminous skirts clutched in her hand.

"There she is," an excited reporter shouted. "Roll camera!"

"Hey, Mimi," a cameraman called, awkwardly giving chase as she sprinted down the long sidewalk toward the street. "Take off your veil."

The bride hopped into a flashy green convertible parked along the curb, switched on the ignition, then gave them a jaunty wave as she peeled out into the street.

The news vans followed. So did the journalists, half of them pulling out cell phones to call in the story. In two minutes, they were all gone.

Another minute passed, then the church bells began to ring. The pealing of joyful chimes filled the air as the doors opened wide and Mimi and Garrett hurried out of the church, ducking their heads to avoid the shower of rice raining down on them.

Once inside the white limousine, Garrett pulled Mimi onto his lap, pushing down the full organza skirt of her wedding gown and giving her a soul-searing kiss. "I wish we could just skip the reception and proceed straight to the honeymoon."

"I know," she said, resting her head on his broad shoulder. "But we have to be there for the grand opening of the LeeAnn Larrimore Mothers' Garden."

Both she and Garrett had been touched by Megan Maitland's wedding present to them. A beautiful garden at the Maitland Maternity Clinic, dedicated to the Lord children's birth mother, LeeAnn Larrimore. It had been completed just in time to be the site of their wedding reception.

"I wouldn't miss it," Garrett said, tracing one finger over her cheek. "I just wish…" His voice trailed off, and he looked distracted for a moment.

Mimi knew exactly what he was thinking. Despite the fact that he'd finally come to peace with his past, his mother's disappearance still gnawed at him. She hoped someday he would find the woman he could never forget.

Then his expression cleared, and a mischievous spark lit his eyes. "Are you ready for your wedding present, Mrs. Lord?"

"Say it again," Mimi breathed. "Just the last part."

"Mrs. Lord?"

"Hmm. I like the sound of it."

He reached under the seat and brought up a square box wrapped in shiny gold paper and topped with a matching bow. "Then I hope you'll like this even better."

She settled into his lap, then opened the box. Inside lay a red leather book with gilt-edged pages. Almost identical to the old journal she'd found in the barn. "Oh, Garrett. It's beautiful."

"You can record every detail of our lives together." He kissed her, breathing in her unique, evocative scent. "Well, maybe not *every* detail."

She laughed, then looked at him, tears shining in

her eyes. "I love it. Our children will love it. And our grandchildren. And our great-grandchildren. It will be part of our legacy."

"I hope you don't mind," he said as the limo pulled up in front of the Maitland Maternity Clinic, "but I already filled out the last page."

She opened the book to the last page. What she read there made the tears in her eyes overflow and spill down her cheeks. Written in Garrett's strong, distinctive script were these words, *Garrett and Mimi Lord lived happily ever after.*

A knock on the shaded limousine window made them both jump. Garrett opened the door to find Bettina Collingsworth, still dressed in a white wedding gown.

"I don't know how we'll ever thank you for playing the decoy," Garrett said, climbing out of the limo, then shaking her hand.

"The exclusive story is thanks enough." The reporter beamed at them. "Now scoot, before those other reporters arrive and try to scoop me."

Garrett and Mimi hurried around the Maitland Maternity Clinic to the back, where a quaint stone path led to a beautifully secluded garden.

Most of the wedding guests were already there, waiting with champagne toasts and good wishes. Then there was the wedding cake to cut and the tossing of the bouquet and garter. Garrett took his sweet time sliding her pink silk garter down her leg to the wolf whistles of the men in the crowd.

Mimi danced first with her husband, then with her father, who beamed with pride. A dance with Michael followed, then one with each one of the Maitland men. After the tenth dance, she'd thrown her wedding shoes into the fountain and danced barefoot.

Two hours later, Mimi finally found some time to herself. Time to relish the happiest day of her life. She looked slowly around the beautiful LeeAnn Larrimore Mothers' Garden, a lump in her throat.

"Thank you, LeeAnn," she said as the stone fountain bubbled behind her, "for loving your son enough to give him up. Otherwise, I might never have found him."

"You're welcome."

Mimi turned to see an old woman, stoop-shouldered and gray-haired, seated on the bench by the fountain. No, not old. Probably not more than fifty. But very frail. And obviously ill. Mimi found herself looking into eerily familiar eyes.

"Mrs. Larrimore?" she said at last, her knees shaky.

The woman nodded, then leaned forward and whispered, "Maybe I shouldn't have come. I just…I just wanted to see my children one last time."

Mimi sat next to her on the bench. "I'm Mimi. Mimi Lord."

"My little Garrett's wife." The woman reached for her hand and squeezed it. "Would you mind introducing me to my son?"

Mimi smiled. Little Garrett was six feet, three inches of solid male. But obviously, in LeeAnn's eyes, he'd always be her little boy.

"Nothing would make me happier." Mimi stood up, then helped LeeAnn Larrimore rise to her feet.

She found Garrett in the gazebo, with Michael, Shelby, and Lana gathered around him. Their laughter echoed across the garden, and Mimi could hear a sob catch in the woman's throat.

"My babies." LeeAnn leaned heavily on Mimi's arm as they stood outside the gazebo. "They're all grown up. They're all so beautiful."

"I know they'll be happy to see you."

"I almost died that day," LeeAnn murmured, unable to take her eyes off her children. "The day I left them here. My husband had passed away three months before, and we were destitute." She shook her head. "I tried to find work, but I didn't even have enough money to pay a baby-sitter. I tried to hang on as long as I could, but the triplets needed milk. Garrett had a terrible cough and needed medicine."

She looked at Mimi with a plea for understanding in her eyes. "I couldn't sit back and watch my babies suffer."

"I know," Mimi said, her own mother's heart contracting painfully in her chest.

"I almost asked for them back." LeeAnn's bony frame began to tremble. "I stood on the Lords' doorstep two years later. I had a good job. An apartment. Enough money to provide the basics. Then I heard voices and children's laughter in the backyard." She stopped and swallowed hard. "One of the girls called Terrence Lord…*Daddy*.

"It's so clear in my mind," she continued, her voice wistful, "even after all these years. *'Daddy, Daddy, push me higher.'*" She looked at her four adult children, laughing together in the gazebo. "And I did the second hardest thing I've ever done in my life. I walked away again."

LeeAnn turned to Mimi, uncertainty clouding her eyes. "Was I wrong?"

"You loved them. That's never wrong."

Awareness prickled the back of Mimi's neck. She looked into the gazebo and saw all four of the Lord children staring at her. Or rather, at the woman standing next to her.

She could see the battle of emotions reflected on their faces. Uncertainty. Confusion. Hope.

Reaching for LeeAnn's hand, she walked with her to the gazebo. The older woman stumbled once, then regained her balance and squared her shoulders, obviously preparing herself to face whatever reception awaited her.

Garrett, Michael, Shelby and Lana all just stared at her. Not one of them said a word. For one brief moment, Mimi feared they might turn away.

Then Garrett stepped forward. "Mama?"

LeeAnn Larrimore slowly opened her arms. In the blink of an eye, all four children were embracing her. Joyful sobs filled the air, some feminine, some masculine.

LeeAnn couldn't stop touching her children, caressing Lana's hair, wiping the tears off Shelby's cheeks, smoothing her hand over Michael's shoulder, tenderly cupping Garrett's square jaw in her palm.

"My babies," LeeAnn cried over and over again. "My precious babies."

Megan Maitland came up behind Mimi and wrapped her arm around her waist. They both stood back and watched the reunion with tears in their eyes.

Megan gave her an affectionate hug. "Don't you just love happy endings?"

"This isn't the end," Mimi replied, her heart overflowing with love for her husband and her new family. "It's just the beginning."

▼ SILHOUETTE®
SPECIAL EDITION™

AVAILABLE FROM 21ST MAY 2004

SHOWDOWN! Laurie Paige

Seven Devils

Zack Dalton had thought he knew Honey Carrington. It wasn't until he had her home in his arms that he started to question who she was…and what secrets she was harbouring.

THE SUMMER HOUSE
Susan Mallery and Teresa Southwick

Two women, two past loves and a tranquil retreat by the sea. Mandy Carter had thought her ill-fated marriage to Rick Benson was over, but maybe things have changed… And when Kyle Stratton turns up next door, Cassie Brightwell realises her schoolgirl crush is still going strong!

HER BABY SECRET Victoria Pade

Baby Times Three

Paris Hanley would do anything to protect her baby, including working for Ethan Harlington. But would Hannah's handsome daddy work out the truth? And would he ever be ready to be a part of their lives?

BALANCING ACT Lilian Darcy

One look at Brady Buchanan's baby had convinced Libby McGraw that she was her daughter's identical twin. She told herself she was only marrying Brady to keep the girls together, but she couldn't ignore what her heart was telling her.

EXPECTING THE CEO'S BABY Karen Rose Smith

Within weeks of discovering a medical mix-up, Jenna Winton found herself married to Blake Winston. The self-made CEO always got what he wanted, and now he was consuming her dreams…even though she couldn't be certain of his love.

MAN BEHIND THE BADGE Pamela Toth

Winchester Brides

Robin Marlowe wanted to put the past behind her, and she had good reason not to trust men like Charlie Winchester. But Charlie was determined to be anything she needed, because he wanted nothing less than her heart!

0504/23a

AVAILABLE FROM 21ST MAY 2004

Sensation™

Passionate and thrilling romantic adventures

SHOOTING STARR Kathleen Creighton
LAST MAN STANDING Wendy Rosnau
ON DEAN'S WATCH Linda Winstead Jones
SAVING DR RYAN Karen Templeton
THE LAST HONOURABLE MAN Vickie Taylor
NORTHERN EXPOSURE Debra Lee Brown

Intrigue™

Breathtaking romantic suspense

ROCKY MOUNTAIN MAVERICK Gayle Wilson
HER SECRET ALIBI Debra Webb
CLAIMING HIS FAMILY Ann Voss Peterson
ATTEMPTED MATRIMONY Joanna Wayne

Superromance™

*Enjoy the drama, explore the emotions,
experience the relationship*

A BABY OF HER OWN Brenda Novak
THE FARMER'S WIFE Lori Handeland
THE PERFECT MUM Janice Kay Johnson
MAGGIE'S GUARDIAN Anna Adams

Desire™ 2-in-1

Passionate, dramatic love stories

SCENES OF PASSION Suzanne Brockmann
A BACHELOR AND A BABY Marie Ferrarella

HER CONVENIENT MILLIONAIRE Gail Dayton
THE GENTRYS: CAL Linda Conrad

WARRIOR IN HER BED Cathleen Galitz
COWBOY BOSS Kathie DeNosky

The employees of the Lassiter Detective
Agency are facing their toughest case
yet—to find their secret desires.

Diana
Palmer

MOST WANTED

SILHOUETTE®

Available from 21st May 2004

Available at most branches of WHSmith,
Tesco, Martins, Borders, Eason, Sainsbury's
and most good paperback bookshops.

0604/047/SH79

FREE!

4 Books
and a surprise gift!

We would like to take this opportunity to thank you for reading this Silhouette® book by offering you the chance to take FOUR more specially selected titles from the Special Edition™ series absolutely FREE! We're also making this offer to introduce you to the benefits of the Reader Service™ —

- ★ FREE home delivery
- ★ FREE gifts and competitions
- ★ FREE monthly Newsletter
- ★ Books available before they're in the shops
- ★ Exclusive Reader Service discount

Accepting these FREE books and gift places you under no obligation to buy; you may cancel at any time, even after receiving your free shipment. Simply complete your details below and return the entire page to the address below. *You don't even need a stamp!*

YES! Please send me 4 free Special Edition books and a surprise gift. I understand that unless you hear from me, I will receive 6 superb new titles every month for just £2.99 each, postage and packing free. I am under no obligation to purchase any books and may cancel my subscription at any time. The free books and gift will be mine to keep in any case.

E4ZEE

Ms/Mrs/Miss/Mr ....Initials....................................

BLOCK CAPITALS PLEASE

Surname...

Address...

....

....Postcode ....

Send this whole page to:
UK: The Reader Service, FREEPOST CN81, Croydon, CR9 3WZ
EIRE: The Reader Service, PO Box 4546, Kilcock, County Kildare (stamp required)